CRIMSON RIVER

N. B. AUSTIN

CRIMSON RIVER

THE CIVILANDS SERIES: BOOK 1

MOORE BELL

~

In life there are mountains that stand before us.
We either reach their peaks or we fall helplessly down.
Yet, the challenge isn't to navigate them safely.
The real challenge is figuring out who we are and why we
climb as we make our way up.
Today my next mountain stands before me, and I'm ready
to scale it,
because even though the destination is covered by clouds,
I've finally discovered my "why."

This book is for people who haven't yet found theirs.
Keep climbing.

~

CHAPTER 1

THE RIVER WHITE

Jeannie Morrell stumbled through the thicket that morning more than she ever had previously. Though her thirteenth birthday had only come and gone about a month before, she was far more familiar with the forests of the Riverlands than most. Still, whether out of fear or fatigue, her short, lean legs continued to fail her. With each misstep, she felt the men drawing closer in their pursuit.

Weaving meticulously left and right through the towering, snow-covered trees, she pressed on. She could hear the hounds just behind her; they crashed through the forest, chasing her as the men at their backs cheered them on, yelling obscenities with a drunken furor. The group was so loud and vile that it was nearly impossible for her to tell the men apart from the barking dogs. With each wide trunk she passed, she considered stopping to try and hide, but she knew there would be no hiding.

Her pale, frostbitten cheeks stung with the same fiery bite of the flames that had engulfed her home earlier that morning. The scent of the smoke remained with her. As painful as those reminders were, she promised herself that they would stay with her and fuel her revenge.

As the voices began to grow clearer, she suddenly burst through

1

the tree line and emerged upon the banks of the River White. Though she had never crossed the river at this time of year, she plunged ahead, willing to do anything to escape the men behind her. Her first step into the freezing water was slow and excruciating, but she knew the consequences would be far worse otherwise. With the white caps of the current crashing upon her, Jeannie furiously swam her way across the river.

Once she exited the water, the winter air produced a chill she could no longer ignore. She swiped at her short, brown hair, which was plastered to her wet face, and gathered the skirt of her soaked, baggy dress, ready to launch into another sprint.

"There's only one way this ends child," a man shouted across the river.

They were upon her.

Jeannie whipped around, her dress throwing droplets of water around her in the process. She quickly counted eight men and four hounds staring at her across the bank. The group was standing behind a tall, thin man who was clearly the leader. The men continued to holler at her, the dogs echoing them by barking viciously in her direction. While those behind the leader appeared to be nothing more than filthy farmers, the leader was dressed quite elegantly. There was, however, no disguising that underneath that thin veneer of wealth he was one of them—the ugliness of his face and his lack of hygiene matched that of his men.

Jeannie stood frozen as her mind gathered all these details, ready to continue running but too horrified to make the first move. The leader silenced his eleven beasts, a dark grin on his face.

"You don't have to meet the same fate as the rest of your Morrell horde, my dear," he continued through tobacco-stained teeth. "You see, my family shows graciousness to those who surrender without too much trouble; crossing this here stream though? Now that's something I'd consider to be far too much trouble. Why don't you come back on over here and we can discuss said graciousness?"

Smoke rose in the distance above the trees from where the Morrell home once stood. Shivering, teeth chattering, Jeannie tried to ignore the tears that began to fill her eyes.

"There was no graciousness shown to my family, and I know there will be none shown to me," she cried. "Why should I trust any member of the Keagan Gang after what you monsters have done?"

The leader took a step forward and looked down at the bloodstained double barrel that he cradled like a child in his arms.

"My dear, sweet, little bird!" he shouted back. "I'm not entirely sure you know who you're speaking to. I'm not just a member of the Keagan Gang. I'm Keagan blood. My name is Walter Keagan, first cousin of *the* William Keagan, and if there is any fish big enough in our humble little pond that might keep his word it is I. That mess back there at your home, it was just a misunderstanding. But you better believe that I would not intentionally harm a precious little lady like yourself."

"Well, Mr. Walter Keagan, my name is Jeannie Morrell, daughter of Adonis Morrell, and you'll have to carry me kicking and screaming back across this river if William Keagan ever wants to see me!" she declared, surprising herself.

She never knew she had such courage in her until that moment, but she didn't have time to think on it as she turned and ran.

As she darted into the trees on the other side, she heard Walter

Keagan's parting shot: "Can't say I'm completely upset with that response. Now, boys, the bird flies! Let's hunt!"

*

The winter was droning on for Hanzah. Being the son of a V'ahani Chieftain had its perks, but the opening months of this year's snowfall had been largely uneventful. At the moment, his father, Chieftain Arkouda, was holding a meeting with his council to discuss provisions for the remainder of Murrieta's harshest season. V'ahani culture dictated that the eldest son stay close to their father at all times to learn from the council, so, as usual for such meetings, Hanzah and the eldest sons of the other three councilmen of the Riverlands were present.

"My dear friends," Arkouda began powerfully with a smile peering through his rough, weathered face. Though only in his late forties, Hanzah felt that his father aged faster than other councilmen, the weight of his responsibility lining his face. "As the snow continues to fall, we must maintain our focus on the well-being of our people. Food, shelter, and clothing must continue to be our greatest incoming trade sources in the months to come."

Boredom was common for Hanzah in such meetings, yet he could not help but look upon his father with confidence at the statement. His father always cared for their people first, above all things. So Hanzah tried to show his support by correcting the hunch of his lanky frame into an upright, straight-backed position. He truly was thrilled that one day he would be the one addressing the council, and he wanted that enthusiasm to be clear.

"It is often that I have wondered what value my words even

have within this council," responded a slouched, younger member of the council in a shrill voice. "This plan for provisions is nothing new. For years we have worried solely about these things, and for years we have paid no mind to the ever increasing violence by the men of the East."

The councilman, who Hanzah knew to be about ten years younger than his father, was named Lennox. Though the members of the council were a tightly knit group, Lennox was known to be more progressive and consistently voiced his disdain with the political stances of the V'ahani as a whole.

"My father was killed under these very same circumstances," he continued. "It is simply the calm before the storm, and we must prepare for attacks in times of vulnerability such as these."

To the right of Lennox was Parish, who was near Lennox in age.

"Um, I agree," he stated.

It was all too common for Parish to agree with Lennox—or anyone for that matter. He was typically very adamant about what it was he agreed with but never seemed to have an original opinion on things, which had always bothered Hanzah.

Parish continued, "Their greed increases with each passing winter, and we frequently experience thieves or outright attacks on our clan members who are away from camp. I have spoken to other V'ahani groups throughout the Territory about it, and we are the first line of defense here in the Riverlands. We must remain strong."

Though the sons of the councilmen rarely spoke their support for their fathers, especially in times of council disagreement, it also wasn't something they tried to hide. Hanzah knew that he was no exception to this unspoken rule, even though he was the youngest son, only having just hit his fourteenth year. It was almost as if a conversation between the sons was being had with the angry looks they shot each other.

"I understand your frustration fr—," Arkouda replied.

"Do you now?!" Lennox questioned with a laugh.

"As much as you do not seem to see it, yes I do," Arkouda said, speaking over and nearly returning the favor of interruption to his councilman.

Hanzah was infuriated by the disrespect Lennox showed.

"We agreed to lead the Riverlands together and the key to fending off threats will be strengthening the alliances we have formed with our trading partners from the East," Arkouda said. "They will be able to influence their own more than we will be able to with guns. At the same time, we do have enough weapons and will continue to use them to defend ourselves. Adequate provisions for our survival must be the most important focus though. The Mother is unforgiving when Her children are not prepared."

To Arkouda's right was his closest confidante beside Hanzah himself, Castor. Castor was the oldest of the group, with about five years on the Chieftain. He looked it, too, with a short but thick beard that was as white as the mess of hair protruding from under his winter hat.

"I must say Arkouda," he submitted in an aged, raspy voice. "This is the way of our people, of that you are correct, and we have seen the wrath of the Mother when we found ourselves unprepared for her rage. However, the Easterners have no fear of Her." He paused, sighed deeply, and then continued, "They are foolish yes, incredibly foolish. They will continue to perish in much greater numbers than we do for this reason. But there also seems to be many more greedy men than we can truly comprehend continuously voyaging into the Territory. I hope that you might at least consider that we prepare for the terrors that they may bring, as the Tokali have done."

Arkouda looked to his friend with a raised brow and replied, "Castor, I must say I am surprised to hear you take this stance. You know the Tokali face circumstances far different than our own. They also rely almost entirely on Eastern weapons while they wonder why it is they face no greater odds. The Tokali know nothing of the power of the Mother, and it has not helped them."

Lennox snickered. "Yes but can it not only help us to have more weapons of war, as well? What are we to do when She does not respond with our grizzlies? Should we not have more guns for the day in which She is temperamental?"

Arkouda quickly retorted, "We will do just as your father did. I saw him fall, and I tell you he was as strong as five Eastern men. We V'ahani are one with the world around us. Trust in that as he did, and together we will fend off any threat." Lennox crossed his arms with a grimace as Arkouda finished, "We will continue the current trade arrangements as they stan—"

A ruckus outside the council chamber interrupted Arkouda.

The leaders looked to one another, then, as one, they lifted their weapons and rushed outside. Hanzah followed hurriedly, pushing his messy, dark hair out of his face. Two V'ahani shifted away from the crowd and came swiftly to the Chieftain.

"Chieftain Arkouda," one began, "we were calling to the wind to conduct reconnaissance and received word of a lone wanderer in the woods. It seems that he is armed."

Arkouda looked sternly at them.

"Take us there, and call to the grizzlies," he replied. "We will deal with this swiftly."

The guides led the councilmen and their sons into the forest beyond their camp. Hanzah was accustomed to the occasional Easterners wandering too deep into V'ahani territory and was somewhat pleased that something entertaining had come along. Though he knew the potential for danger that the Easterners posed, seeing the V'ahani grizzlies in action was always a thrill.

After some time charging through the snow-laden woods, the guides began to slow to a stalking pace. They motioned to their leaders to do the same. Hanzah felt the exhilaration of a hunt as they crept along. Finally, they spotted their target in the distance.

The heavily layered character wielding a gun moved slowly but urgently. It was in moments like these that Hanzah came to appreciate that his people dressed in all white. It blended in so cleanly with the snowy Riverlands, and that camouflage represented their superiority over their realm. Just when Hanzah inferred that this person was on a hunt of his own, the figure lifted his rifle in the air. Hanzah followed the line of the rifle to see it was aimed at several deer with massive antlers that were calmly grazing in the distance.

Just then, Arkouda murmured to the men, "Make the call."

The first guide began to whisper, and soon a distant crunching of branches could be heard. The wanderer in the woods lifted his head from the sight of his rifle. In that moment of hesitation, the deer instantaneously ran off. The figure turned back rapidly toward the location of his meal that wasn't to be, when suddenly the initial crunching of branches turned into a thunderous pulverizing of the forest floor.

In no time at all, a massive grizzly towered over the poor soul, knocking him to floor and smacking the rifle out of his reach. Hanzah soaked in the massive image of power that had been on display before him, but the next part was always the most difficult to watch. The bear took two swipes at the wanderer, the first of which tore through his many layers and the second of which ripped the skin across his chest. The wanderer screamed out in an agony that brought Hanzah no joy.

It was difficult to see the stranger's wounds with the grizzly now roaring and standing on its hind legs in front of him, but through the gaps, Hanzah spotted a dark orange color. His shock was met by gasps from the V'ahani with him, and the bear soon calmed into a heavy, winded panting. Just as the V'ahani were identified by their white clothing, the Tokali were known for their orange.

"Do you all see his orange?" Arkouda whispered, confirming everyone's thoughts. "He is of the Tokali."

"What would you have us do, Chieftain?" one of the guides asked.

The Tokali figure now lay in the snow, still conscious, but frozen in place and fortunate that the swipe was not worse than a flesh wound.

"Send the bear off and go fetch him," Arkouda answered. "We will take him back to the camp and find out what he is doing here. Be sure to remain on guard in case there are more of his people behind him."

The guides nodded and marched over to the scene of the incident. When they arrived, they initially stared down at the man sideways. Then, one hoisted up the young man's rifle and knocked him out cold before binding him and dragging him back to their camp.

There were so many thoughts rushing through Hanzah's mind on their return. Why had a Tokali traveled this far north when there were clearly so many risks he could face? Was he somehow unaware of the historical tensions between their clans and of his proximity to the V'ahani Riverlands camp? He'd heard that the Tokali placed less emphasis on the bloodline connection that the native clans had with nature, but did this man not know or fear the grizzlies of the V'ahani? He was eager to find out.

When they returned to the camp, the young Tokali's eyes began to open. A group of clan members who had spotted his orange garment soon began surrounding and berating him. Hateful words were being thrown in his direction, along with kicked dirt and stones. Through the mob Hanzah could just make out the cowering figure of the young man, who appeared similar in season to his older sister, Latera. An undeniable sense of pity soon arose in him.

"Seems the grizzlies roughed this one up a bit!" one man proclaimed.

"Let them finish him," another added. "This maggot has no place here!"

Arkouda quickly rushed toward the mob and, with a dagger firmly in his hand, lifted the pile off of its feet. "Tokali filth!" he howled, moving the blade to the young man's throat. "What business do you have this far north?!" The mob began to echo and cheer him on. "How far behind are your Tokali companions in their attempt to attack us?!"

By the looks of it, the young man could hardly breathe. He was wounded in multiple places, the worst being his head and chest. The only reply he could muster was a cold, vacant plea for water. His desperation became apparent, and the crowd hushed.

"Let him go, and we will tie him up," Lennox called to Arkouda. "He is clearly not our enemy; perhaps the tides are turning."

As much as Hanzah appreciated his father's protectiveness, it seemed Lennox was right. The man was no threat in his current condition. Arkouda reluctantly accepted and followed the request. However, the tension of the V'ahani around him remained. As they dragged the Tokali man to a cell, Hanzah began to realize this would be no ordinary winter.

*

With a Tokali man now occupying a cell in the Riverlands, there was great unrest at the V'ahani camp. As Latera went to meet with her father, whispers passed all around her, carrying great confusion. In her twenty years, she'd never heard such spreading of rumors and speculation amongst her people.

"They are not to be trusted, we should execute him, there is enough to worry about with the Easterners," one man snarled along the way.

Another responded angrily, "This is exactly why we must unite with our brothers and sisters in the south!"

Latera turned her head sharply left and right as opinions were hurled around, disturbing her long, braided hair. Though she grew frustrated to have to keep fixing it, and though she knew better than to show such ardent interest in public, she could not help but listen in. Each voice spoke in a tone as if it was of the utmost authority and reason, speaking in disgust over those who would dissent. Latera felt troubled by the way they simply disagreed in outrage rather than making any attempt to understand why the opinions of others were formed. That path only led to discord—and trouble.

After plodding through the noisy camp, she finally reached the council chambers. When she entered, she spotted her father pacing slowly, his hands behind his back and his head tilted downward. Arkouda's long, thick hair was a dense black, which had become lightly peppered with gray over the years. Today, Latera seemed to recognize the gray more than usual.

"You summoned me, Father?" she asked, while casting a quick look around for Hanzah.

Though Hanzah was six years her junior, Latera remained very close with her little brother and wondered where he was in this moment of upheaval. She spotted him sitting silently in the corner, just where he should be. He gave her a quick little nod in greeting.

"Yes, I did," her father replied. Latera whipped her eyes back towards him and found him looking up at her. "I must make an important request of you Latera. I need you to tend to the prisoner before we interrogate him. You are to clean him up and stitch his wounds."

Latera's main occupation was tending to the wounded, something she learned from her late mother, when V'ahani men returned from all types of scuffles. However, she was surprised and nervous about her duty in this case.

"Father," she replied, "After the stories you have told of the Tokali, you trust me to be in there with him?"

"I would never let anything happen to you, especially because of the stories I have told," he warmly responded. "You are simply well equipped for this task, and you will be accompanied by a guard who will ensure that you are not harmed. I also need to trust that whoever goes in there will not berate the young man! Can I trust you to get him cleaned up for me, my love?"

"Yes, of course, Father," she nodded and bowed toward him. Then, casting a quick, uncertain smile toward her brother, she turned to leave the chamber, flanked by a large, armored guard.

When Latera arrived at the cell, she saw similar wounds on the Tokali as those she had seen on many of the Easterners whom her people had also broken. She walked slowly over to the sulking body with her supplies. His hands were tied to a pole behind him, and she could not see his face, which was covered by a head of unruly black hair that fell to just before his shoulders.

"Are you awake?" she asked nervously.

The young Tokali man sharply lifted his head and began breathing heavily, as if her sultry voice had been a monstrous roar. Latera was so startled that she fell back off her feet. Initially, he seemed to be more afraid than she was, but as he looked around, his breathing began to calm. When he was settled, he whipped his hair out of his face and looked at her directly in the eyes with a slowly expanding grin. Yet, despite the grin, his most noticeable feature remained his eyes, which were a brightly colored hazel that reminded her of the forest just at the beginning of the fall season.

With his gaze still fixed on her, he softly said, "I am awake, and I am badly hurt, but I am more so happy that such a beautiful woman is now before me and not a tremendous bear."

She successfully hid her appreciation of the compliment as she kneeled down to get a better look at his wounds. "I see the grizzlies got to you," she said with a pleasure she did not attempt to hide. "What is your name?"

"Yes, one did," he replied. "I am just grateful it did not kill me. We down south were unsure if the stories of the V'ahani bears were even entirely true. They will not believe me when I tell them that I escaped one!" His bright expression quickly faded back into a grimace as Latera cut off his shirt. "Oh, and my name is Elan. What is your name?" he added just as she had opened her mouth to respond.

"Escaped? Not with this foolish orange your people wear. Plus I suspect the shimmer of your eyes alone would give you away in our forests. No, if you survived our grizzlies, it was only because we allowed you to," she said, trying her best to remain stern despite her enjoyment of the conversation. She began to examine his wounds, attempting to look past how well built he was beneath them, and gathered her supplies to commence the stitching. "But tell me, why are you here, Elan?"

"No name, I see," he joked coyly. "And I cannot disagree about my eyes in these snowy woods, but I am also looking at a woman whose eyes are likely the lightest blue in the entirety of Duresia, let alone the Murrieta. They are so beautiful and clear, they are nearly white!"

Latera could feel herself blush as she finally smiled.

"Ah, there she is!" He paused, admiring her, before continuing, "To answer your question as to why I am here, the Tokali are struggling in the south of the Territory. The lions of the East show us no mercy, and we have had great difficulty for years defending our lands the way your people can. We do not frequently utilize the gifts of the land like the V'ahani do, nor are we as skilled with weapons as the Easterners. Though we have great numbers, theirs seem to be infinite, and they are not as scattered as they once were. The real reason I am before you is that I was sent by my people to deliver a message. The Tokali wish to unite. We *need* to unite, or we will not survive, and when they finish with us, they will come for you."

Latera could not believe her ears. She had always buried herself in her work as a nurse to avoid the stresses of politics, but she realized she was now the only V'ahani to have heard this important message. This time, it was her eyes that fixed on his.

"The lions of the East? Of what do you speak?"

"The men who wear the symbol of the lion with pride but are snakes slithering into our lands."

Latera paused, processing his meaning. "Our clans have been enemies for years, Elan," she said, her guard now completely down. "Did your people really believe you would succeed when they sent you here?"

"We had no choice," he responded with a seriousness she wished she had maintained. "And something tells me your people do not have one either."

These were the last words spoken for some time. The only sound made between them was Elan's wailing as Latera commenced stitching his clawed skin back together. Once she finished his chest, she moved on to the gash on his head. Lastly, she tended to some final wounds he said he'd sustained at the northernmost Tokali camp he passed through along the way here, when Easterners attacked.

When it was finally over, she began to wash the blood off of his body and face. After he was cleaned, at the attention of the guard, he redressed into new clothes and tied his messy hair up into a bun. His new clothes, however, were V'ahani white.

Looking downward in awe, he exclaimed, "I never thought I would be wearing this color!"

"You should rest," Latera said with a grin. "Some men will be coming soon to talk to you about what you have told me. If what you say is true, then I sincerely hope our people can unite. There is no longer a place in the Territory for violence amongst the native clans." She turned to leave the cell but quickly stopped. "Oh and by the way, my name is Latera," she chirped and continued out.

When Latera arrived again at the council chambers, she told the gathered men all that she'd heard. She enjoyed being the news bearer and could tell the entire council was in disbelief. She listened as they discussed how and if it could be true. Such an alliance could be quite the defensive asset against the Easterners, certainly, but they remained skeptical. The clans had been enemies for longer than anyone could remember, and a proposal from one's long-term foe was bound to make anyone suspicious. Latera herself wondered why the Tokali would make this decision now, and why they would send a young man along with such an important message, but she knew the councilmen would be sure to find out as they all descended upon the cell.

They filed in one by one: Latera, Arkouda, Hanzah, Castor, Lennox, Parish, and the other sons.

They soon took their places, and Arkouda started, "I heard what you have told the nurse. You understand this is very puzzling news. Our clans have always lived apart, and relations have never been well between us. Why do the Tokali now wish to form an alliance?"

As Elan looked upon the great councilmen, Latera watched him and noticed a new, bright light entered his eyes.

"First, my friends," Elan started. "May I say thank you and introd—"

"No," Arkouda interrupted. "I do not necessarily care who you are yet. First, you need to explain to me the reason why we should believe what you say is true—for that matter, why we should keep you alive at all. We could have easily had that grizzly finish the job, yet we spared you. Prove to me why that was wise."

"Oh I know that you *could* have, but you must already know a reason why you stopped him, correct?" Elan replied foolishly.

"Yes," Arkouda scoffed. "But we can bring him back in here right now if that is what you would like, though I would assume you would not want to go through that again—so, back to my question. Be careful to answer without the arrogance you are spouting. Why now, Tokali?"

Latera held her breath, wondering if the young Tokali would be foolish twice.

But Elan only sat up straighter and with a deep breath explained, "Certainly, Chieftain, my apologies. As I mentioned to the gracious young nurse, the men of the East who have inhabited the central lines of the Territory are growing stronger. Their previously scattered gangs have formed a more compact union, which has been trying to muscle its way into our lands in the south for some time now. It seems to be their intent to control all trade in the Territory. This new gang is not like any that came before, either. It has grown so vast that they may soon reach this goal, and then they will likely continue north. If that happens it will not be pleasant for you. Their armies are unnaturally violent—our outposts have suffered at their hands."

His face took on a beseeching look, and he took a deep breath before continuing.

"Chieftain Arkouda, this is why we *must* come together. We must stop this threat before they conquer the entire Territory. These men will enslave us and do all measures of worse things if not. The Tokali have seen it all firsthand."

Those in the room took a moment to process the revelation that Elan had laid before them.

The silence stretched until Castor spoke, "But how do you know for sure that the men intend to move north once the south is won? Surely they know the harshness of the conditions up here."

Latera cast a quick look Castor's way. The look of doubt on his face was reflected in the faces of the other councilmen.

"Our villages have been destroyed," Elan responded somberly. "Our people have heard them state their plans as they rode through our homes." He paused for a moment, as he choked up and eased his fingers through his hair. "I was in one of those destroyed villages on my way here," he continued. "I only narrowly escaped, and I saw the direction this particular gathering of men was headed. They rode north, same as me. With their dogs, with their horses, and with their guns. It was not their full force—of that I am certain—but they are coming. They know of the wealth that exists up here in your lands, and they want it for themselves. They want the whole Territory for themselves."

Castor turned pale, sitting back in his seat, and whispered, "Then it is as we feared."

Latera felt her stomach twist at his words.

"If you are right about these Eastern men," her father started, "then it appears we should gather our forces to stop them. However, we must take some time to consider what you have said. The V'ahani have never made peace with the Tokali. I will be damned if we do not discuss the implications of this decision first."

Latera knew her father to always remain patient and firm in his stances—even now, when others were despairing, he remained strong. Elan nodded in understanding.

Then Lennox chimed in, "This new union of Easterners that you mentioned, what do they call themselves?"

Elan looked around the room. Latera could feel the anticipation in the cell and with the attention of all on Elan, he replied, "They call themselves the Keagan Gang."

*

"I believe this to be an obvious choice; in fact, it should not be a choice at all." Lennox began, pacing around the room with urgency.

By the fact of his youth, he was the most animated of the councilmen and also the best kempt, both of which had likely contributed to his quick rise through the V'ahani ranks.

The council had left the Tokali's cell and returned to the chambers for a meeting that would ultimately determine the future of the V'ahani clan. Hanzah understood the gravity of the situation and listened intently as Lennox continued.

"For the sake of the survival of the great clans of the Territory, the V'ahani must come to the aid of and unite with the Tokali, despite any historical differences. We must take this boy south immediately and speak to his people. We can send word to our brothers and sisters in the Mountainlands at the Great Fortress and at Orrin's camp that we will do so. Like Elan has told us, these Keagans will not stop until we are at their heel, and you all saw what they did to him. You heard what they have done to his people, and with the great opportunities in the North, we will be no exception—with or without the help of the Mother."

Hanzah could see that the other councilmen agreed with Lennox, and a knot of worry began to form for his father, who Hanzah knew did not agree.

"My friends," Arkouda started, looking first to Lennox. "I am the Chieftain of our great branch of the V'ahani here in the Riverlands. This was the marvelous honor entrusted to me when I took my oath at the Great Fortress, in front of the Grand Chieftain and his Masters." Arkouda stood behind Hanzah and rested a hand on his shoulder. "This is our future. We are the first line of defense. What would happen if we were to take this journey and fail? What if we were ultimately unsuccessful without having first sought the approval of our leaders? This mission south you speak of is not ours to assign. A meeting with the entirety of the V'ahani in the North must be our first step. We must bring Elan to the

Fortress and let our leaders decide."

"Your position here is exactly what makes you fit to accept this as our only choice, Arkouda," Lennox angrily battled back. "You should have the authority to make such a decision in order to defend your people. There is simply no time to waste. We should send word of our intentions to the Fortress, of course; however, if this boy was truly intersected by the Keagans and is with us now, then how far behind do you think they must be?"

Castor added, "The hard truth is that the journey south to the Tokali is much easier traveled than to the Great Fortress in this winter. We all know what the conditions will be on the way up and across the river, never mind what it will be like to take all of our people through the Mountainlands."

"Yes this is exactly right, through the Mountainlands where we will cross my brother Orrin's camp on our way for support and sanctuary," Arkouda pleaded. "That is also one more group of our own people than if we traveled south immediately."

Hanzah stood still and straight, supporting his father as best as he could in his silence. There was a slight pause when everyone looked at one another.

"I think we should show that we have spine," Parish countered. "The element of surprise could be a great advantage against the Easterners. The boy seemed to believe that they did not know of his escape. So they currently think they will be the ones hitting us when we are not ready."

"This is the case indeed, Parish," Lennox warmly agreed. "If we send word north now and group with the Tokali in the south, then our people can send men from one direction while our unified force strikes from the other. We would essentially strangle the Keagan clan."

Everyone waited for the Chieftain to speak again. His was always the last word.

"You all make great points, so we will continue this discussion tomorrow afternoon following the morning hunt. This will help us clear our minds for the final decision. I still believe we are best suited to a strategy of strength in numbers with our own people and letting the Grand Chieftain and the Masters lead us to a fight if necessary. But until then, we will ask for the Mother's guidance in this decision."

The other councilmen departed with their heads hung. The council was not a democracy but an advisory, so when the Chieftain made a decision, it was typically final. Everyone knew that the strategy chosen would be Arkouda's—and it would only be made official the next day.

*

The morning hunt among councilmen and their sons took place once a week on the first day of the week. Though the V'ahani hunted with great frequency, the weekly council hunt was a tradition. Each councilman brought along a rifle that they taught their sons to use proficiently, week after week. Hunting for deer and bison was occasionally mixed with fishing along the River White.

The men brought their fishing gear the following morning and planned on bringing back a feast worthy of such a momentous day. As soon as they entered into the forest to the northwest of their camp, they got to work. The sons took turns calling up to the wind to gather their bearings on the positions of the beasts they sought. Deer roamed far and wide this time of year, and they were quick to discover a herd of bucks. The boys took turns downing their prizes through the morning, one at a time, missing their targets on several occasions. After a few hours each boy had bagged a commendable trophy, with the guidance of his father. They then passed off their rifles to the four fathers of the council, and the group made their way through the forest to the river for some fishing.

Arkouda and Hanzah walked ahead of the others and talked.

"Father," Hanzah said, "Why does the rest of the council wish to make the journey south despite the truth that you speak? Do we not need the assistance of our people?"

"We are a very strong group here in the Riverlands, Hanzah," he replied. "We have hundreds of able-bodied men in our camp who would be an asset to any army. The councilmen feel the way they do for this reason, and for that I cannot disagree with them. We would not be trusted with the Riverlands if we were unable to fight." The edge of the forest and flowing river beyond it came into sight.

"However, these Keagans do not sound like any other threat we have had to deal with from the East," he said. "Not only must we unite our people first, but we must unite all of the North, including our eastern allies, so that the Keagans do not beat us to any of them. Unity is our greatest asset, but we must start with those we know for sure will fight by our side. I am not yet certain the Tokali will fulfill that criteria based solely on the words of this young man."

Hanzah nodded at this, wholly agreeing with his father not

simply because he was his father, but because the logic was sound—and safest.

A few moments later, they heard a ruckus in the distance. The other councilmen caught up and gathered close, taking cover behind some nearby trees. When they identified that the noise was coming from the river, the men lifted their rifles and the boys their hunting daggers. Hanzah recognized the howls ringing in the air.

"Hounds," Lennox whispered to the group, voicing Hanzah's thought.

They began creeping toward the edge of the forest. When they eventually reached it, they took cover behind the final tree line. A small figure from across the way could be seen exiting the forest on the opposite side of the river. After a pause, they saw the figure jump into the water.

By this point, Hanzah inferred the obvious: this person was escaping the chasing hounds. Arkouda pointed to a position for cover by the riverbank, upstream from the figure's position in the water.

"Move to the bank, we can hide there," he whispered, and they quickly followed his order.

Once in cover, the councilmen aimed their rifles toward the opposite side of the river. Soon enough, a group of men burst out of the tree line. The escaping figure had made it to the other side of the river, and Hanzah could now see it was a young girl. He squinted a little harder and soon realized he knew who she was.

"That is Jeannie Morrell," he alerted the group with a start, fearing for the safety of the girl, with whom he was fairly familiar.

The men looked his way and then promptly back down the sights of their rifles.

Voices could soon be heard, though a hundred yards or so away and mostly muffled in the winter winds. The only audible phrase soon came with a loud cry from Jeannie.

"Why should I trust any member of the Keagan Gang after what you monsters have done?"

A response echoed from a tall, ridiculously dressed man, "I'm Keagan blood. My name is Walter Keagan, first cousin of the William Keagan . . ."

And this was all the V'ahani needed to hear. Even if Jeannie Morrell hadn't been recognized to be their ally, the enemy was now clear.

"Our foes certainly like to dress up as easy targets," Parish joked.

"I have known Jeannie Morrell since she was just a toddler," Arkouda noted. "She is the daughter of Adonis. By the smoke rising above the trees, I take it the Keagans discovered the prominence of the Morrells in this region. We must defend the girl."

"Maybe these Keagans did us a favor," Lennox said. "Once we lay waste to their gang, the wealth of the North could rest solely with the natives once again."

"Even if that is so, Adonis is a friend, and the girl is innocent. Boys, call to the grizzlies," Arkouda ordered.

Hanzah swelled with pride at his father's decision and at his own role in it.

Just as Hanzah and the other sons began their ritual, Jeannie scurried into the tree line, and Walter Keagan clearly shouted, "Now, boys, the bird flies! Let's hunt!"

The men and hounds began their obnoxious cheering and howling once again.

Hanzah continued calling to the grizzlies, knowing that the councilmen would wait for the Keagan Gang to cross to their side of the stream. The hounds were the first to emerge and sprinted toward a tall tree that Jeannie had climbed up into. They carried on barking ferociously up at her. Just as Jeannie began to cry, the crashing started through the woods. Hanzah specified his instruction and was relieved to see the two tremendous bears barreling toward the tree. The dogs attempted to retreat with a whimper, but the bears were too swiftly upon them, tearing each bloodhound apart limb from limb.

With the gang having nearly cleared the stream, his father and the other councilmen began to fire their rifles. When the first rounds were delivered, two men went down. The rest hurriedly attempted to climb over one other and onto land, but by the time the second shots rang out, three more had been hit. The blood of the fallen spattered on the survivors like paint being sprayed onto a canvas. One of the men was shot but not killed and tried desperately to grab the others for assistance. However, he was promptly shoved off and struggled to remain above the surface of the water. Hanzah was disgusted by the lack of honor in these men, but he made sure the emotion did not interfere with his task.

Hanzah watched as Walter Keagan, completely out in the open on the riverbank, used his remaining two men as cover as he moved toward the trees. They each pulled their weapons and began firing wildly in the general direction of the councilmen and their sons. Then the councilmen fired the fourth and final round.

One shot went straight through a defender's chest, sending him reeling backward to the ground. Another bullet hit the other man's leg, going clean through his calf and into Walter's behind him.

With the hounds finished, the grizzlies soon assembled onto the bank per the boys' instructions, keeping Jeannie behind them, still up in the tree. The man who was still blocking Walter Keagan was screaming in pain like a dying animal. He cursed the clan with every obscenity, none of which as ugly as he was, with his scruffy, untrimmed face. Then the councilmen came out of their cover and began walking toward the pile of bodies with their rifles now drawn and reloaded. When the screaming man saw them, he continued hurling words with ever increasing vulgarity their way.

Hanzah looked toward his father. Arkouda nodded back at him. With great pleasure Hanzah began his ritual once again. The first grizzly proceeded to the Keagan man and, after letting out a great roar, bit into his skull, crushing it with its powerful jaws. While Hanzah did not often revel in the violence of the grizzlies, this time the pleasure was undeniable. It felt satisfying to stop these men who were against his people and going to hurt Jeannie. In that moment, his duty felt like an honor. The boys then sent the grizzlies back off into the woods as the councilmen descended upon Walter Keagan.

With a dark grin, Walter chuckled uncomfortably. "Quite the specimen y'all got there! I always did think it a silly myth what people said y'all could do with them bears. I'm sure glad to know the Keagans will soon control y'all and those powerful beasts."

"What are you doing here?" Lennox demanded, just as Arkouda opened his mouth to reply.

"Oh, I think y'all know the answer to that already now dontcha?"

Walter sneered, though his struggle with the pain was obvious. "With the North comes the spoils in the Murrieta, and my family would very much like those spoils for ourselves."

"There will be no family for you much longer, only death," Arkouda submitted gently.

Hanzah looked sharply at his father. So the Keagan would die then. Then it would be best to start collecting the weapons strewn over the bank now. He signaled to the other sons, and they slowly moved around the group, staying close but steering clear of the Keagan's reach.

Walter climbed up the bank to get as comfortable as he could, given the circumstances, before answering.

"Well, I'd say that makes two of us, my indigenous friend. Your time has come. I take you to be the leader . . . and for what you did to me here? Shit. My cousin Clovis is just back through those woods across the river, and he'll be looking for me—you can bet your woodland ass on that. See this here Lion's Paw pin? Well, it's our Keagan pride."

"A pin is your family's pride?" Arkouda interrupted. "Ha, how trivial."

"Trivial as it may seem to you, now every one of us wears it on our chests, and I can guarantee that it'll be one of the last things you see before you die. Soon they'll fill the Murrieta, bringing fear with them far and wide. If I were you, I'd be hoping it isn't Clovis that gets the honors of showing it to you for the last time. As for your people, they'll come to know the symbol very well. The Keagans will have full control of the Morrell trade routes very soon. Y'all will do business with my cousin William, or you, too, will die."

"The Mother will determine our fate, Walter Keagan, not you or your people," Arkouda calmly replied.

"Adonis Morrell and his brood are dead, short of that there girl up in that tree. She has a ton of value if returned to my cousin though. Alive, I might add. She's needed and will not be harmed by us, if that gives you tribesman any peace of mind. William will also provide a handsome reward for my return, and, seeing as y'all know the wealth once possessed by the late Adonis Morrell, I take it y'all know the significance of the word, 'handsome,' in this case."

Arkouda's head tilted. "You cannot save your life Walter Keagan. You are right about the girl remaining unharmed, but wrong about your family having any sort of control."

Hanzah watched as Arkouda lifted his rifle and walked slowly toward the unfazed man.

"Stop!" Jeannie suddenly yelled.

Hanzah froze mid-reach for another shotgun and looked on in amazement. Jeannie, having climbed out of the tree when no one was paying her mind, began running toward the men.

"He's not yours to kill," she said.

She came to a halt in front of Arkouda and looked into his eyes directly. "If you had any respect for my father, you'll give me that rifle and allow me to avenge his death."

Arkouda receded with a bow, "Fair enough. I cannot deny your request."

He lightly dropped his weapon to the ground and backed away toward the water. Jeannie was slow to approach at first but soon began reaching for the rifle.

Hanzah was wondering if she'd take the shot when Lennox

spoke, "There has been a change of plans. Boys, take Hanzah and the girl."

One of the sons ran toward Jeannie and subdued her while the other two came at Hanzah. Luckily, he was able to trip one of them up and pushed the other to the ground, avoiding their clutches. Jeannie was not as fortunate. She began screaming and demanding to be set free. The councilmen then lifted their guns at Arkouda. Hanzah let out a shriek of his own, the sound retching from his throat. With three shots that he felt were loud enough to shake the entirety of the Riverlands, they each put a bullet inside the abdomen of his father. Horror and betrayal were etched onto Arkouda's face as he fell dead into the river. That look was the last thing Hanzah saw before he instinctively turned and dived deep into the water, allowing it to carry him downstream.

CHAPTER 2

OUR FEAST, THEIR FAMINE

William Keagan sat at the head of the table, staring down at nothing in particular, as was his typical habit whenever he wasn't speaking. What precisely he was staring at in these moments he knew to be a topic of endless debate for those who knew him. Perhaps they were curious because his contemplation was often accompanied by what they described to be an angry, snarling look on his face, a look that seemed to say the thing he was staring at was "so repulsive to behold that William challenged its very existence."

For those who dared to ask him about this habit, a group limited to his siblings, he had explained that he wasn't staring at any particular thing, nor was he angry. Yet, for some reason, the curiosity of those around him persisted. Others had always told William that in many ways his personality was contradictory—and that itself fueled their interest. In fact, those who knew him best had frequently professed that they could not decide whether they preferred him to be calm or furious, as either tended to be unsettling. His brother Daniel had even once described him as a majestic, inviting volcano that could explode at any moment, or not explode at all. William found these opinions rather entertaining.

The Keagan dining room was somewhat infamous for its décor,

the table set so elegantly that a guest would temporarily forget that he or she was still in the heart of the chaotic Murrieta. William had done this intentionally, though admittedly somewhat ironically, as the Keagan mansion and the town of Fayette in which it was located was positioned almost directly in the center of the Territory.

Tonight, the people sharing his table all sat silently. When they had entered, William was pleased to see that they were dressed in a fashion that was as remarkable as the room, and, for a moment, he'd thought that if they never spoke, they could have easily been confused as decoration.

When the meal finally came and was served to the table, William chose to break his trance by passing a hand over his beard, which was trimmed just enough to be considered clean-cut without being overly proper.

He looked up, lifted his silverware, and with a polite smile said, "My humble guests, let us begin our feast."

In unison, his guests all followed suit, lifting their utensils, and politely digging in.

The entrée was William's favorite meal, roast pig—a fact made obvious by the presence of the head of the animal on a large plate at the center of the table. William made sure that the display faced his seat at the head of the table. He felt it important that he always face the lives he had taken, whether directly or indirectly, believing he owed it to the fallen as a courtesy.

To William's right, seated in a row, were the men of his closest inner circle. The man who had been by his side since the day he left for the Murrieta, Gregory Calloway, held the first seat. Gregory was a middle-aged, balding beast of a man who could break a person with his bare hands. He was a great ally and had been ever since swearing his undying loyalty to William, who had saved his life in the past. It was an investment that William never regretted.

The next seat belonged to Daniel, the middle Keagan brother. All three brothers, separated in age by three-year increments, had left their home in the East together with nothing and now stood at the head of the most prominent gang in the Murrieta. Satisfaction filled William at the thought, before greed reminded him that they needed to further expand their influence into the final piece of the Territory, the all mighty north, to truly be all powerful in the region. Daniel spoke to William about these things every day. He still raved about all they had achieved under William's leadership and about his own pride that he could help his brother oversee their trade routes.

Of the three brothers, Daniel was the most socially aware and could convince most people to sell him everything they owned within the span of a short sit-down and chat. His good looks hadn't hurt in this regard, either, as women back east had always ogled over his shiny smile and thick, well-maintained hair. Daniel always wore it slicked back, which William thought went well with his business-centered personality. Though William wondered whether occasional jealousy crept into Daniel's thoughts, William was extremely thankful to have a brother so loyal and knew he couldn't have made it so far without him.

The next two seats currently sat empty, but typically were held by his youngest brother, Clovis Keagan, and his cousin, Walter Keagan, respectively. Clovis was a clever, extremely animated young man who was a perfectionist with a depraved longing for violence.

The combination of these traits made him quite an effective military mind, something that William unrepentantly utilized in his strategy. As Clovis's twenty-ninth birthday was only a few months away, William had recently "gifted" him the permission to lead their territorial expansion. Clovis had thanked him sincerely and profusely for the "freedom." Walter, who was himself two years younger than Clovis, was a thrill seeker and common companion of Clovis's on his conquests. He was electrified by conflict, yet he prided himself on his politeness in conversation.

The final two chairs along the right of the table belonged to William's fifteen-year-old cousins, Blanton and Donna Keagan, who were identical twins and Walter's younger siblings. The twins were constant companions, even at this late age, primarily because Donna had an odd social condition in which she could only speak as a follow-up to her twin brother, finishing a sentence of his own. Unlike the rest of the family, who were tall and thin, the redheaded twins had not yet grown to their full height and were overweight, a fact that led them to be clumsy. Walter and the other Keagan brothers were defensive of them in the face of others, but that didn't stop William from finding most everything about them comical in his private mind. Walter's parents had not seen the humor in these characteristics, however. Instead, they had become entirely frustrated with the twins, which was what had landed the twins in the care of their brother and cousins.

"Who are our guests then, cousin?" Blanton asked William, indicating the people sitting to William's left and breaking the silence that had resumed at the table.

"Yes, Billy, who is this exquisite lady sitting beside you?" Donna echoed.

William finished chewing and answered, "Well children, these kind folks next to me are the Abigale family. This fair maiden to my left would be the lovely Judith Abigale."

William watched as Judith blushed at his remark. The two had only been introduced once previously, but William was pleased with her beauty, to say the least. She had long, silky hair in a reddish-brown color, which incidentally was his preferred coloring in a woman. Her figure took an hourglass shape, emphasized by her red corset and dress, which only intrigued him further.

"Sitting next to Judith is her father, Henry Abigale, then her mother, Maria Abigale, then her sisters, Henrietta and Florence Abigale, and finally her youngest sibling, her brother, Francis Abigale," he finished.

"And uh, what business does the Abigale family have at our table?" Blanton followed up with a mouth full of food.

"Now Blanton, don't be rude," chirped Donna.

William was pleased she had corrected him. "Hard to understand what you're trying to say when your mouth is so stuffed, but there is no business here today, my boy, only pleasure." He looked back to Judith with a smile as he continued his lie, "This is the woman Walter and I told y'all about, the one I'm to marry, thanks to Mr. Abigale here."

"Oh no, William, the pleasure belongs to Mrs. Abigale and I," the father added politely. "You'll make a fine husband to our Judith." Mr. Abigale paused and took a bite of food before continuing. "Might I ask by the way, of the whereabouts of your brother and cousin? I do hope they'll be able attend the wedding in a few days!"

"That isn't none of your business, so no, you may not ask," Gregory coldly replied, staring directly at the now-frozen Mr. Abigale.

William trusted Daniel to best put people at ease and cut him a quick look. Daniel rested a hand on Gregory's arm and coolly corrected William's beast in response.

"Gregory, please. Mr. Abigale, you're a guest in our home. Soon you'll be family here, as well. You may ask whatever questions you'd like. Clovis and Walter are currently away on business in the North, trying to seek out new trade alliances for our family. They should be back in time for the wedding. You see, I coordinated their expedition, and I assure you that we planned it with every intention for that to be the case. They certainly didn't want to miss it, either."

Mr. Abigale's tense shoulders visibly relaxed again. "Well who would?" Mrs. Abigale chimed in merrily. "In the Murrieta we must take every opportunity for joy we receive, mustn't we?"

William smiled. "Most certainly, Mrs. Maria. By the way, might I ask how you're enjoying the meal my chefs have prepared this evening?"

First dabbing her lips with her napkin and chewing the remainder of what was in her mouth, she replied, "Oh it's delicious, William, send them my regards. They must be the best in the Murrieta!"

"I'd say they certainly are—and if they weren't, they would be replaced by the ones who were." He turned to Judith. "No expense will be spared for this angel's happiness, I can assure you of that. I don't believe there's a more charming face in the west to face me at the other end of my table every night."

It was one of William's decided traditions, and he had thought up many, for his wife to sit at the opposite end of the table, at the other head, during meals, but to only do so once officially married.

Judith continued to blush, before replying, "Thank you, William. Your words are too kind."

The group continued eating quietly for another few minutes.

"So where are y'all from? Are you from the East like us?" Blanton again blurted out.

"Of course they're from the East, only the native clans are actually from the Murrieta," Donna answered.

Suddenly, young Francis looked up, his face suggesting that a light had just turned on in his mind.

"Why are you doing that?" he asked, looking at Donna.

She looked at him angrily, but did not say a word.

"Francis, silence!" his father interrupted.

William was not bothered, however. He knew Francis was too young to understand the social dynamic of not being a Keagan at the Keagan's table.

"Father, I'm sorry, but I'm simply confused," he squeaked, too ignorant for his own good. "Why does she only speak after her brother speaks?"

Donna's face was now nearly as red as her hair.

"Don't you worry about it, little boy," Blanton said, showing Francis his size with his body language.

William nearly chuckled out loud at the display.

"You're so lucky my big brother Walter isn't here," Donna grumpily followed.

"See!" Francis simultaneously replied pointing at her.

Henrietta and Florence giggled.

"That's enough!" Mr. Abigale yelled at his son. "I'm so sorry, William. He will learn the meaning of respect tonight, I can assure you of that!"

William looked toward Donna, who was now on the verge of tears.

"Oh don't apologize, Mr. Abigale. I suspect you are right anyhow," he replied, sending a smile in Donna's direction.

He gave her a wink that calmed her down, and she finally smiled back.

"No more of this foolishness!" William declared. "I'd like to propose a toast, to my beautiful soon-to-be bride and to our brothers beginning our venture into the North. May both journeys be prosperous, and may they lead to many more feasts, such as the one we have devoured this evening!"

The group raised their glasses in unison before sitting back down and falling into silence again. Dessert would be coming out next. Until then, William opted to retreat back into his trance, his own mind being so much more interesting than the company. He stared down at his empty plate.

*

Soon after Chieftain Arkouda was shot in front of her and she'd watched his body fall onto the bank of the River White, Jeannie ceased resisting capture. She no longer contained the will to fight—not on this day, when all that she knew had seemingly vanished. What remained was nothing but smoldering timbers, blood, and kicked-up sand. Staring into the now murky water of the river, she numbly wondered what was next. As if in answer, the young men surrounding her yanked her forward, forcing her through the woods and back to the V'ahani camp.

She vaguely recognized that the councilmen—that's who she assumed they were anyway, being that they'd been with the Chieftain—at least had the decency to walk her apart from the now-hobbling Walter Keagan. One of them, who appeared younger and more aggressive than the others, lagged back to walk near her and the boys.

"You and your family had seen them before today, had you not?" he asked, nodding toward Walter. Jeannie gave no reply, so he grunted and walked ahead again.

But his question had brought up the memory, even if she was unwilling to share it. And almost against her will, a day from a few weeks before, the day she'd first seen a Keagan, sprang up into her mind.

Each Monday, her brother Harrison, who was the eldest of her two older brothers and five years her senior, would go into town to trade supplies with the locals. Their father had made Harrison responsible for the route about two years prior. After receiving his parents' permission, Harrison decided to take her and their brother, Donovan, along with him one Monday—to introduce them to the role and what it entailed.

Harrison's route cut through the town of Harran, which was part of the Riverlands and nearby to the Morrell home. Harran was one of the few relatively safe communities in the Murrieta, thanks to the consistent stream of goods running through it and its mostly peaceful relations with the nearby V'ahani—both of which were facilitated by their parents.

Jeannie had always known her brother to take pride in his work, so she was unsurprised when he had explained the process to her and Donovan with great enthusiasm.

"The people around these parts rely heavily on our family, and it's our duty to deliver their needs each week," he began as he gathered his goods for the day. "I head into town and take requests for goods for the coming week, and then I deliver the orders that were placed last week."

"Do you ever have any problems with bad people?" Donovan interrupted nervously.

Jeannie hid her smile. Donovan wasn't quite as brave as Harrison yet.

"Not yet," Harrison said. "But our father is well-known and well-liked around these parts, so I don't anticipate it happening. In case it does though," he added, after a slight hesitation, "here's a pistol for each of you. We'll go out back for some target practice before our run."

Jeannie hadn't ever been allowed to shoot a pistol before, and she wondered whether Harrison had gotten permission for this, too. They practiced shooting for an hour or so, pretending the targets were this criminal and that criminal. Throughout their session, Harrison provided them with tips on how to improve their accuracy until he decided it was time for them to get on their way.

On their arrival into Harran, Harrison put Jeannie in charge of taking the next week's orders, so that he and Donovan could focus on delivering the previously ordered goods. Both Jeannie and

Donovan were able to meet several townspeople in the process, and on their way home, Jeannie asked Harrison about several characters that had piqued her interest.

The first Jeannie asked about was Charles Langston, an oafish man who was the self-proclaimed mayor of Harran, which was unusual considering that Harran was not even a properly organized town. Harrison told her that at one point, the man even falsely claimed that the community had elected him to the position at a local gathering and that he "reported" to governing forces outside the Murrieta. He was clearly delusional, Harrison told her, but since he seemed to be mostly well intentioned, most people let him be—especially since his stories were entertaining no matter how untrue they seemed.

Then, after a little prompting, Jeannie had cajoled Harrison to tell her about Cassie and Debra Kennedale, the sisters who claimed to be joint psychics. To the shallow men in town, the sisters, who were each in their upper thirties, were not viewed as particularly attractive. Their faces were littered with freckles, they had awkward smiles that intentionally hid crooked teeth, and their blond hair seemed to fall from their heads more than it flowed. The younger of the two by a few years, Debra, took their lack of attention harder than the thick-skinned Cassie. However, it did not keep either of them from being extremely kind to those they cared about, and Harrison mentioned that their home was always a favorite stop of his. Harrison explained that they made a good living convincing men on their way through Harran that great fortunes awaited them in the Murrieta. Much to their amusement, the men whose futures they "foresaw" largely never returned to dispute them.

Jeannie laughed when Harrison shared this, thinking the sisters terribly clever.

The last townsperson Jeannie had wanted to know more about was Dominic Turner, and she made it clear that she was especially excited to hear what Harrison had to say about him. Mr. Turner had made a coin disappear and reappear before her eyes earlier that day when she was taking his order, and the man had fascinated Jeannie ever since. Just as Harrison was about to get into his story, however, a tall figure rode up to the siblings on horseback and interrupted him.

Jeannie's first thought at the time had been that the man did not look like most people in town—now she knew he was nothing like them.

"Excuse me children," he beckoned, his accent foreign to her. "If y'all could help me figure out where I am, I'd greatly appreciate it seeing as I'm not from these parts. Would these be the Riverlands?" he asked through a large, toothy smile.

"That's right, sir," Harrison replied. "What's your business here?"

"My business?" he asked. "Well I have no business here yet, but I'd very much like to."

There was a charm to him, Jeannie thought. But since out-of-towners were never to be trusted, she remained on guard at Harrison's lead.

"Do y'all children know how close we are to one Adonis Morrell, as a matter of fact? I hear he's a man of great skill in these parts who I'd very much like to talk to."

Jeannie didn't like that this man was looking for their father. It wasn't unheard of, of course, for people to want to meet Adonis

Morrell, but this man was stranger than any who'd come before him. Jeannie took a close look at him then, noting his frilly clothes and, in particular, the garnish, gold lion's paw pin that was pinned to his coat. What an odd thing to wear.

"Fairly close," Harrison finally answered uneasily.

"Well, children, don't look so tense!" he said in a far jollier tone than Jeannie had heard anyone in the Murrieta speak. "Y'all have been a great assistance. I'll be on my way now. Stay safe!" He then turned his horse around and rode away with alarming haste.

There were no more stories of the townsfolk as she and her brothers headed straight home, unease skidding up their spines.

If only she'd known what the lion's paw pin meant that day. If she had, she thought, her family might still be alive.

Looking up, she realized they had made their way through the forest and nearly arrived at the camp, which was just ahead. On arrival, the men rushed her through the camp into a small building. Ordering her inside with a single guard, they held a muffled conversation that Jeannie couldn't hear outside before entering.

The councilman who questioned her earlier approached her and coldly explained, "We know who you are, and we will ensure your safety, but we need to hold you for a bit for our own protection against the Keagans. I am very sorry for what they did to your family."

"Don't lie, please," Jeannie muttered. "I know you aren't sorry, and what you did was horrible."

The councilman's face scrunched up for a few seconds.

"Did you and your family see them before today?" he asked again.

"Yes, we did, but not the same ones that came today," she replied angrily. "Why? What difference does it make? There's no way we could've known this was coming."

"That would be where you are wrong, child," he declared in a louder tone. "I knew this was coming. I knew it, and I did not even know who the Keagans were until a day ago. In fact, the Keagans were not even the catalyst of the thought. No, this was inevitable from the time you and your Easterners first came into our territory. And now, look what has become of it. This is not just about the gangs and the murderous wanderers. The Morrells are just as responsible for the position in which my people and I have been placed. For the decision I had to make."

"Don't you dare blame us for your cowardly decision!" Jeannie roared back.

"Cowardly? My decision was anything but cowardly!" He shouted, his face becoming flush, veins appearing on his forehead and neck. "Once we have rooted you people out of our lands, it will be perfectly clear that we did what was necessary to survive!"

With that, he turned and stormed out. The guard stood by the doorway in silence, and as much as Jeannie resented the councilman, and as much as she saw the truth about the greed of the Keagans, she couldn't help but wish that he could see the difference between her family and that cruel gang.

*

The pace of the current was beginning to pick up. Once Hanzah knew he was out of sight of the councilmen, he burst to the surface of the river and gasped for air. His arms flailed listlessly and soon grew heavy from fatigue as he was pushed down the rapids. He tried desperately to swim toward the edge of the stream, but the current was too strong. On an attempt to surface his head, he saw a tree branch hanging over the crashing water in the distance. It appeared to him to be just low enough to grab onto, and he merely hoped it was thick enough to hold his weight. He started swimming less to preserve his energy, steadily moving closer and closer until he was within striking distance. Once upon it, he used all his weight to jump upward out of the water, his right hand reaching for the branch. His hand landed, but his grip failed him—too weak to compete against the thundering waters. He felt himself slipping until he held onto nothing and crashed back into the water. At the next turn, he was thrown against a rock. The sharp pain in his head was the last thing he felt before everything faded to black.

Sometime later, Hanzah opened his eyes. His vision was blurry, and his head was pounding in pain, but he quickly realized he was no longer in the ice-cold river. Thankful he was now lying on the shore, he lifted his hand to his head, which he could feel was wrapped in cloth. With his awareness still returning and his body shivering violently, he recognized the presence of someone sitting beside him, carving away at an apple. Once he felt in control of his functions again, he jumped up and knocked the carving knife out of the man's hand.

"Who are you?!" he yelled as he backed away. "Where are we?!"

The man did not move in response, which gave Hanzah the opportunity to look him over. This was a man of the East, and in a way, that actually put Hanzah at ease. After what had transpired earlier that morning, he was afraid he wouldn't be able to trust any of his own. Behind the man, Hanzah spotted a horse tied to a post and some camping equipment hanging over the saddle. There were also several other items he did not recognize, so he returned his gaze to the man himself, who wore a curious looking hat that covered his curly blond hair. The man appeared to be dressed somewhat formally. Yet his clothes, though well to do, were slightly worn down, and the very beginnings of a beard shadowed his face. He appeared to be about the age of Lennox, Hanzah thought.

The mysterious figure peered up at Hanzah from underneath his hat.

"Well, that there is my horse, Nala," he replied. "As for me, I'm a man that saw a boy struggling in the water. I followed that boy and recognized that he needed saving, so I saved him. Who are you? And how does a young V'ahani fall into the River White at this time of year?"

"I did not fall. I jumped," Hanzah replied defensively. "Thank you, though. Thank you for saving my life. What can I do to repay you?"

"Well I'm pretty sure there's nothing you can do to repay me for saving your life, but I have been wrong before. Anyhow, you can start by handing me my knife off the ground, so I can continue enjoying this apple," he answered.

Hanzah could tell the man was much less simple than his demeanor suggested, but he said nothing. Instead, he lifted the knife and handed it over.

The man got back to work on the apple and said, "Thank you. Now you can tell me who you are and why you jumped into the River White."

"My name is Hanzah. My people . . ." He trailed off, struggling to retell the tale, struggling to even comprehend that his father, the Great Arkouda, was dead.

The man rested his knife and looked up, prompting him to continue. Hanzah thought to start with what was clear to him, first.

"There is a very real danger coming to the North," Hanzah said. "A young Tokali came to warn us of them. Then we chanced upon some of them by the river while on a hunt. My father is—" he paused, his voice having broken on the last word, "was the Chieftain. His councilmen wanted to join the Tokali to stop them. He only wanted to do what was best for his people, but I believe the councilmen saw an opportunity to achieve their own goals and so—and so they killed him. They must have been planning it. Somehow, I escaped."

The Easterner took a deep breath, staring right ahead for a moment, before looking at him. "I'm sorry, son. That all sounds horrible. But, did you say your father was Chieftain Arkouda?"

Hanzah nodded.

"I knew of him. He seemed an honorable man from what I heard." The man paused and then looked back up with fire in his eyes. "When you say 'them,' you're speaking of the Keagans, aren't you?"

"What do you know of the Keagans?" Hanzah asked with sudden alarm.

"Don't you worry yourself," he replied. "I'm certainly not a friend of theirs. They're the reason I'm on my current path. It was my intention to leave the Riverlands and possibly the Murrieta altogether. They came up here and did unspeakable things to my town, so I gathered a few essentials and left the rest behind," he said sadly.

"We were a tight knit community in Harran, and it's one of the few homes I've ever had where I felt truly accepted. There simply isn't a place with as many quality people in the Murrieta— or anywhere for that matter—as Harran. Those bastard Keagans came and burned down the home of the very people that held it all together for us. Very generous, they were. Unfortunately I've heard that none survived."

Hanzah felt puzzled at first, but began connecting the pieces. "Are you from the same town as Jeannie Morrell?" he asked.

The man beamed. "Yes, Harran! Did you know Jeannie well?" he asked, excitedly.

"I knew her before, yes, but I have also seen her today. She is alive," Hanzah smiled briefly. "But my people have her, as well. I suppose they believe her to be very valuable."

"Jeannie's alive!? My goodness that's great news, Hanzah!" the man exclaimed. "The entire Morrell family is invaluable to the Riverlands, and I, in particular, owe them my life. You see, when I first decided it was time to leave the East of Duresia and cross the Chorisma River into the Murrieta I was excited but terrified. Then I got here, and I discovered how right I was to be afraid. Crossing in was obviously hell, but finding peace once I made it through was also a challenge. Gangs were everywhere then, and, like many others, I unfortunately found myself a part of one, simply to be around other people who could keep me safe. For a while, that's all it was, but soon our gang grew, and its leaders became greedy. They started asking things of us we weren't comfortable with, and, eventually, they wanted me to kill a man in a rival gang. To that point, they'd kept me safe, so I . . . I didn't know what to do."

His eyes had widened through his story, and now the man paused to crack his knuckles.

"Did you end up doing it?" Hanzah asked reluctantly, feeling for the man's situation.

"D-doing what?" the man shot back, still cracking away one-by-one.

". . . Um—di—did you end up killing the man?" Hanzah followed, now on edge due to the man's odd reaction.

The man looked startled for a moment and then glanced away as he continued, "I suppose I had no other option at the time, or at least that's what I told myself. When I pulled that trigger, something happened to me, though. To this day, I'm not sure what to make of it, but all I knew at the time was I needed to escape that life. So I did. I ran away from there, and eventually I came upon the Riverlands, into these very woods in which we now sit. For some time, I was alone and suffering from guilt. I was on the verge of giving up, when one day, while scrounging for food, one of your bears came upon me. I was as terrified as I'd ever been, but at that point I'd accepted my fate.

"That's when Jeannie's father, Adonis, appeared out of the woods and stood in front of that bear as fearlessly as I've ever seen a man be. He couldn't speak to that beast like you natives can, but Adonis had such regard for others that it didn't stop him from protecting me. That brand of goodness is not natural even in the best of men. I imagined his relationship with your people must have been a good one, too, because soon some of yours came around and sent that grizzly along. From there, he introduced me to Harran and its community, which, like I said, was truly a home for me. Now I don't know Jeannie as well as Adonis, but if she is alive, I owe it to him to ensure her safety, the same way he ensured mine for so many years."

He paused and then looked at Hanzah with ferocity in his eyes. "You must lead me to your camp, so we can retrieve her," he demanded. "As it turns out, I was wrong about you. You were wondering how you could repay me for saving your life, well, this is it."

Hanzah was horrified at the thought of going back, but knew he had to try to save his sister before traveling north to his uncle Orrin in the Mountainlands. He was going to make the journey his father had suggested. He was going to warn his people.

"You have a deal," he said. "But I will only return there on one condition. My sister is there as well and we must rescue her, too, if we can rescue Jeannie Morrell."

The man nodded, "Fair enough, my young friend. Lead the way to your camp, and we'll set them both free."

The man stood, but Hanzah remained in place until the man sent a questioning look his way.

"You must tell me your name, stranger, before we travel together."

The man smiled. "Ah, yes, of course. Dominic Turner, at your service."

*

Following the feast, William anxiously paced the halls. He wanted some time alone with his future wife. There were things he needed to say to her—and her alone. Now retired to her room, she was surely tired from the journey into the Murrieta. Though her family had been safely escorted in for the purpose of the marriage, William knew from experience that the trip was long and much more dangerous than what people from the East were used to—especially wealthy people like the Abigale family.

After some time of wandering the halls in procrastination, he finally composed himself and came to her door, where he delivered three knocks.

"Who is it?" she called.

"It's your future husband, my dear," William quietly answered. "May I have a moment of your time?"

". . . Um, of course," he heard her reply after an initial hesitation.

As he opened the door to walk into her room, Blanton and Donna ran behind him, chasing a screaming Francis down the hall. The young boy had a tin bucket on his head, courtesy of the twins, who followed behind him, wielding wooden spatulas they were using to bang on it. William worried slightly that Judith wouldn't appreciate her brother being teased, though he was pleased to see his cousins defending each other.

Taking a step toward her after chuckling briefly at the children, he slicked back his greasy, chin-length hair.

"You know, if everyone were to agree on a mutual sense of humor, I'm certain all strife in the world would be cured shortly thereafter."

A tiny grin cracked through on her face as she gave him a nod.

Then, looking downward, he continued, "Anyhow, I plan to be brief, my lady. I just wanted to say that I'm very grateful that you're here. I don't know what you've heard of my family or the Murrieta or me." He stepped closer to her and his eyes moved upward to look into hers. "Whatever you've heard, though, I will never hurt you, I will never let anyone else hurt you, and you will know all the wealth this land has to offer."

She paused. He nearly held his breath waiting for her response, still uncomfortable around a woman like her. When she looked back at him, it was with a squint.

"May I be frank, William?"

Startled by her unexpected response, he said, "Yes, of course, please."

"Well, I would like to know how ambitious you are," she started. "I come from great wealth and excitement in the East, and I hope I didn't come all this way into this strange place for less than I had before."

William remained speechless as he processed a directness the likes of which he would have never expected from such a beautiful, seemingly proper woman. Apparently he took too long to reply, because she continued.

"My family was provided a great chauffeur named Cassius on our journey, who has been tasked to remain with us. If you can't give me the lifestyle I desire here, then please just tell me now, and I'll have him take us back immediately."

William snorted, and his laugh transformed into a dark grin he could feel spread across his entire face.

"My lady. I didn't expect such . . . honesty. I assure you that you're exactly where you need to be for wealth and excitement. The Murrieta is a wild place. This mansion you reside in, the feast you enjoyed, these are only the beginning of the riches I will acquire in these golden lands."

With that, she edged slowly closer to him, emitting an air of arousal that was certainly mutual.

"Well, then I want you to show me. I do not wish to be the trophy at your table, but the voice in your ear and the woman by your side. Consider nothing off limits for my sensibilities. I would expect to be appraised of your plans and their consequences so together we can shape this place to our vision. Can you promise as much?"

"My lady, if you can promise this fire in you will not fade soft in rough winds, then I swear to you I will feed it. Let me ask you, do you know why you're here, Judith? The real reason?" William asked, thinking he might have a better way to answer her question.

Their eyes locked.

"I'm here to marry you," she answered. "Likely for appearances to those with which you do business. Also, perhaps, for pleasure and offspring."

"You're close," he said, waving a finger at her and feeling a growing admiration of her sharpness. "That's certainly part of the reason and will be an asset as I expand my influence here in the Murrieta. I also have very much always wanted children of my own. But please give me some credit, my darling, I think on a scale much larger than most men. Now, why are you here? I'll give you a hint and tell you that your family has a role to play in this."

She tilted her pretty head, which made her wavy hair fall gracefully to one side.

Taking a moment she added, "Well, my father has influence back east. He could provide connections there, as well."

Affirming her answer with an animated nod, William continued, "Yes and who did your father previously work for in the East?"

Her eyes widened, and she beamed. "Your father. This is about your father," she replied.

Judith would have been well aware of William's father, Leonard Keagan—anyone back east would.

"That is correct," William said solemnly. "My father was surely the one who found y'all that chauffeur of yours as well, wasn't he? Cassius brought y'all here safely over the Chorisma and through Prayer's Passage and remains here to ensure that safety continues. I believe this shows my father clearly places great value in Mr. Abigale, despite the fact that he left the East for the opportunity I offered him here. Your father is one of the few men fortunate enough to have Leonard Keagan's ear. I was never so lucky. He deemed this place to be untamable, and I think he considered me the same way. I will prove him wrong though. Once I take the Mountainlands, I'll have access to more than just riches. We've received word that the V'ahani Fortress is not just for their defense from the south. It also serves as a barrier on the Murrieta side of the only land bridge connecting this land and the East. Because the bridge is so far north, and because no Easterners to see it have ever returned to tell of it, it's entirely unknown to them. When we take the Fortress, we'll open it up, and there'll finally be a safer way to the Murrieta during the summer months—a way far better than crossing the Chorisma and traveling through Prayer's Passage, that's for damn sure.

"If your father becomes an advocate of the work we're doing here, then I believe I can connect the Murrieta with the East. At that point, I'd have enough power to tame even the Passage. The great eastern cities and this territory will no longer be separate entities. A partnership with my father would result in the largest conglomerate this continent has ever seen!"

He paused, stepping up to her so their bodies nearly brushed. "You want wealth and excitement, Judith? My lady, I don't mean to be rude, but you haven't even begun to understand what those words can mean yet."

"Well, William Keagan," Judith whispered sensually as she began slowly removing pieces of clothing. "You have intrigued me. I can promise you I am more than ready to be the best wife I can be for you. Now show me what those words mean."

By the time she was fully revealed, William had closed the small distance remaining between them and slowly wrapped her in his arms. This woman was like nothing he had ever seen, and she was his. Soon, it would all be his, but in that moment, the rest didn't matter quite as much to him. As she accepted his advance, he pressed his lips against hers, and the flame was ignited. In no time at all, the two found themselves tangled in one another. Though he wasn't a virgin, that night was the first time in his life that William Keagan truly made love.

*

Night fell over the V'ahani camp, the atmosphere very different than it had been just days before. Latera knew she should be with the members of the clan, preparing for the outcome of the council meeting, but she'd been in tears and immobile since Lennox delivered the news. Her father—dead. Her brother—dead.

All at the hands of that damned, wretched Keagan Gang. A part of her, the small part that could spare any thoughts beyond her grief, wondered at the reason that little Jeannie Morrell was being watched over by a guard when she was suffering Latera's same loss, her family dead not even a day—but right now, Latera couldn't make it matter.

Almost as soon as Elan had opened her up to the possibility of immersing herself in the larger world, in another clan culture, in a united native world, losing her family had destroyed those dreams. She didn't care anymore. Her typically braided hair was a mess, and she couldn't even work herself up to fixing it. So she just lay there for hours in her sorrow.

That evening, however, she decided to gather what strength she did have to join her people and hear what the councilmen's next step would be. Since his return, Lennox insisted she be accompanied by a guard, who he assured her was there to provide anything she asked for. She tried to tell him it wasn't necessary, but her protests were to no avail.

When the councilmen finally emerged, the V'ahani were all waiting and eager to hear the determination. Parish emerged first, followed by Castor, and finally, Lennox.

"V'ahani!" Parish began, "After much deliberation, the bravery of Lennox in his attempt to save our lost Chieftain Arkouda and his strength in the capture of the monster, Walter Keagan, have led the council to name him our new Chieftain! May Chieftain Lennox lead us to glory!"

Then the new Chieftain Lennox approached the mass of his people in their whites, flanked by Parish and Castor.

With his face lit by fire he began, "My people, in our cell sits Walter Keagan. He is an awful man who, as you know, has killed our fearless leader and his brave son," he furiously declared to grumblings from the group.

Elan was then brought to the Chieftain's side. "This is the Tokali we have taken in, Elan," Lennox said. "He lives and breathes in our camp because we must unite. We must eliminate the threat of the wretched Easterners who create havoc in our lands. The V'ahani and the Tokali must become one to defend our Territory!"

The group gave a cheer of approval to their new Chieftain.

"The Keagans are violent and terrible," Elan added. "My people and I are enthralled by your decision to stand with us against their tyranny. I now ask you to march south so that we may combine our forces."

Lennox built off of Elan's support, "It is decided by this council that we will march south! We will bring this Keagan prisoner as a hostage and alongside the Tokali we will rid the Territory of these greedy outsiders!"

Latera could see that the V'ahani, warriors and civilians alike, were ready to stand with their new leader, and, in a way, she was pleased. She thought that perhaps Lennox was carrying out a decision her father would have made.

Lennox raised his hand for silence. "As always if there are any dissenting opinions from the people of the Riverlands, please let them be stated." He gave the customary pause and scanned the crowd.

Suddenly, Latera heard a pop in the distance from the forest. A light travelled higher and higher into the air as the entire crowd turned and looked on in confusion. The silence was broken when a great explosion burst and filled the sky. Panic and unrest filled the camp as the fire that woke the night took the form of a lion's paw. As the image filled Latera's eye she began to tremble. The symbol of her loved ones' killers made her feel weak. Her mind began to race in all directions, and her heart was beating out of her chest. She fell to her knees and began crying loudly again.

In the commotion, Lennox furiously called out, "Men, take positions! Women and children, to your homes!"

The guard by Latera's side tried to encourage her to follow him back to her home, but she remained on the ground. Lennox rushed over to her and then turned to the guard.

"Get her there now," he demanded. "I want five other men with you as well. Protect her at all costs."

Amid the commotion, Elan ran over.

"I will go with them," he stated. "Latera, come with us. You are going to be all right."

She remained in a kind of shock, but acknowledged his promise and was able to snap to her feet. Elan put his arm around her shoulder, and she followed him along.

In the madness, Latera could see the warriors of the camp had assembled and prepared for the coming threat. They waited for the Keagan force to rear its head and rush from the trees, but rather than a group of attackers, more pops and explosions began to fill the sky. She became taken by the colors of each burst. Never had she seen anything like it, and, despite her panicked state, she felt as if there were explosions occurring inside her, too—ones that were re-shaping her and who she was in her entirety.

When they had reached Latera's home, she peered out an opening to see what was going on. By now she was sure an attack would engulf them in flames, but after about five minutes of explosions and anticipation, it became obvious that an attack was not coming—at least not from the trees. Surely this had to be a diversion, but something still didn't feel right.

In a booming voice, Lennox called out to his men, "First wave, go out into the trees and get to the bottom of this. Second wave, follow closely behind. I need a group of you, with me." With that, off he went.

Then, Latera heard a roaring coming from the woods. She assumed at first that the men were calling the grizzlies, but then she could make out from the distance that a single grizzly was standing against the V'ahani. It did not appear to be fighting, but rather acting wildly. Suddenly, Elan gently pulled her away from her viewing point.

"Please do not worry yourself, Latera," he said. "We will stop them. I will not let them hurt you, I promise."

There was so much going on that didn't make sense to her, but Latera appreciated his bravery anyway.

Not long after the noise began to subside, Lennox rushed in past the guards at the door.

"Are you all right, Latera?" he asked, seeming extremely flustered.

"Yes, I am fine, but what happened out there?"

Lennox seemed to ignore her, looking straight at Elan, who was still by her side.

"So there was no trouble here then? No disturbances of any

kind?" Lennox questioned.

Elan shook his head. "Nothing at all," he replied, to which the other guards confirmed.

Lennox looked away for a moment. "All right . . . yes, that is good to hear," he said. Then he turned back to Latera, "It was no major threat for now. The only mishap was that the guard watching the Morrell girl was incapacitated, and she is nowhere to be found. Otherwise, there were no issues to worry about. The Keagans seemed to truly want her, so they must have come and snatched her up. We were able to secure Walter Keagan though, and there was no loss of life, so we simply must act promptly now that this has passed."

"And what of the bear?" Latera added.

"Seems it was startled by the noise or something initially, but it ran off—and again, no one was harmed," he said quickly. "We must return to the fire and regroup with everyone now." With that, they all followed him out. Once the V'ahani were all back together, he explained the same story he had to Latera.

"Despite what happened, the Morrell girl is not our priority by any means, and with Walter Keagan in our grasp, they are still at our mercy," Lennox added. "As we were saying before, and now what is twice as clear is that the time to act is now! People of the Riverlands, prepare yourselves, for tonight we travel toward unity!"

With that, they all nervously cheered and readied. Latera felt their fears, doubts, and hopes. However, that night had planted a seed inside her, which she had never felt before. Losing her family and seeing her people in disarray made her realize that she was truly in this now, and that she would no longer simply allow herself to be at the mercy of the current.

CHAPTER 3

THE ENEMY OF MY ENEMY

They ran and ran. Back through the woods and onward toward Dominic's campsite, they ran to escape the V'ahani that they had just made to look like fools. For the first time since the attack on her family's home, Jeannie Morrell felt hope. She recognized the man ahead of her as soon as she saw him, and though she never got to hear the story Harrison was going to tell her of Dominic Turner, she felt safe following him nonetheless. Hanzah was also someone with whom she was familiar through their fathers' close relationship.

When the trio finally reached the clearing by the River White, Jeannie took in the makeshift campsite that was already set up and took a moment to catch her breath. Dominic introduced his horse, Nala, to Jeannie and passed around rations of what food and water he had.

"I'm sorry to end our brief rest so quickly, my friends, but they'll be leaving their camp and heading south sooner now rather than later," he said. "We have to move at least a few clicks up the river to avoid crossing their path."

Jeannie nodded reluctantly, then Dominic grabbed Nala and his supplies and they began trekking north along the river.

They walked in silence for a while, still absorbing the events that had taken place, but her curiosity was bursting, and Jeannie could only force herself to hold the silence for so long.

"You're Dominic Turner," she said to the man who brightened at her recognition. "I remember you from Harran. I don't however remember hearing much about who exactly you are. So . . . who are you, sir? If you don't mind me asking," she politely quipped.

"I am interested in hearing more, as well," Hanzah added. "I thought my people were the only ones who were special in the Murrieta. But last night I saw you manipulate fire in the sky. How did you acquire this power, and why have you brought such horrors to the Riverlands?"

"Power!" Dominic laughed. "How flattering! No, I'm what's known as an illusionist. My craft is welcome in the Murrieta by those who wish to be entertained, which is the thing that brought me here. Unfortunately, as an illusionist I can't tell you how I do what I do or it would no longer be special! And then no one would pay me!" he said with a wink. "For now just know that I'm a great fan of your father, Jeannie Morrell. He saved my life in more ways than one, so I consider it my duty to help protect yours in these difficult times. Actually, I admired both your fathers, as I told Hanzah a bit earlier."

"If only I knew of a place you could guide me to," Jeannie said with a frown.

"The only place I want to go now is back there to find my sister," Hanzah also muttered. "She needs to know that I am all right. She needs to know the truth about what happened."

Dominic responded, "I'm sorry, Hanzah. I wish we could've had the opportunity to free her, but there were simply too many men at your home, and that is not your fault. I should have prepared for such a possibility. Perhaps we could try to intercept her on their way, but that might be too difficult."

Hanzah shook his head. "No, that would be foolish," he said. "I just pray she remains unharmed."

Jeannie felt her heart tug for Hanzah's sister, but she suppressed it, as it only made her think of her own siblings, who she didn't have the opportunity to save at all.

"I'm sure she will," Dominic said. "We will find a way to warn her, somehow. Until then, and until we all find somewhere safe, I'll be your guide—and consider it no trouble. You both convinced me that there still might be hope for me and this place! And I owe you a debt for that alone."

Dominic paused a moment, before chiming, "I have an idea! How about I show you a trick, my young friends? Sometimes a sense of wonder can help us escape from hard times, even if only for a moment."

Jeannie felt her mood lighten just a little—maybe Dominic would make another quarter disappear!

"There is no escaping the loss we have had to endure," Hanzah moaned. "You cannot know the pain if you think it will just go away."

"I know I could never understand what each of you must be going through, but please, trust me for just one more moment if you would?" Dominic replied.

Hanzah nodded, and Dominic sat them down in front of him and set up a small platform. On the platform he placed two matches horizontally from one another.

"Two simple matches," he said as he displayed them with his hands.

Dominic then placed his right hand over the right match and his left over the left. He lifted his hands to reveal both matches in the same place. He then flipped his hands so that his palms faced up, and he once again covered both matches. Jeannie grew confused in anticipation as he again lifted to show the matches in the same place. The illusionist appeared amused by the children's reactions and lifted the right match with his right hand. After he revealed it to them, he placed it into his left hand, closing that hand as he did so. Finally, he lifted the left match with his right hand, first revealing it to them and then closing that hand around it. With both hands closed he asked, "Now Hanzah, I'd like you to pick a hand, and I'll give you what's inside. Jeannie will get what's in the other. Be sure to choose very carefully."

"But what is the difference between the matches in each hand?" Hanzah asked, as he reached out to select the left hand.

"There is no difference between them at all," Dominic said with a playful grin. He opened his left hand to reveal that it was empty and handed both matches to Jeannie. "But Jeannie will be able to tell you this for herself, because she will have them both."

Jeannie sat and stared at his hands. "How did you do that? How did you get the first match from your left hand to your right?" She looked up to see that Hanzah appeared to be just as much in awe of the man as she was.

"I understand your need to question but as I said, a magician can never tell," he offered politely. "To remain on a good note, though, I believe we are far enough up the river to be out of harm's way now, children. Let us rest and make camp."

Jeannie was exhausted, so this was welcome news. Once everything was set up, she was quick to plop down comfortably. To pass the time, Dominic told stories about his more exciting journeys through the Murrieta and moments from the shows he had done. Hanzah added tales of his people about their history and particularly of the grizzlies. It was a great relief for Jeannie to learn more about each of her new comrades, and she was glad to see Hanzah begin to relax a bit. She happily listened along and occasionally recounted memories from her childhood, as well.

After a good while of talking and resting, a faint rumbling of voices could be heard coming from a distance up the river. Jeannie was the first to jump up at the sound, though she waited until Dominic signaled for them to quietly march ahead to investigate. As they got closer, Hanzah made a movement, indicating that he recognized their location. They were approaching the banks where the bloodbath from earlier had occurred.

From their safely distanced vantage point, Jeannie noted what must have been close to one hundred men on the grounds of the scene. Several appeared to be searching for clues of what transpired.

"How the FUCK did this happen!?" the leader yelled out.

Jeannie recognized the shrill, icy voice as soon as she heard it. It was the same as the one that led the Keagan troupe on her home. Her heart sank. Now the evil that was Clovis Keagan had a face, and oh what a face it was. Though Clovis was similarly built and dressed as she remembered Walter and Daniel had been, he made no attempt to look as proper as they did. In fact, Clovis's beard and haircut were trimmed so poorly that it almost seemed like it had to be by design, so that regardless of his long, lean frame, he did not look elegant in the least. In a way, despite his distaste with everything around him, there was an atmosphere about him that suggested he knew—and was comfortable with—the kind of man he was.

"These are Keagan men," Jeannie leaned over and whispered to Hanzah and Dominic. "That one, with the fancy clothes, is Clovis Keagan."

"Devin!" Clovis shouted. "What of Walter and the girl? I swear I'll melt the goddamn skin off of whoever's responsible for this."

A figure, which Jeannie guessed was Devin, stepped forward, a swagger in his step. He was not nearly as lavishly decorated as the leader, but was more so than the others and had large, puffy hair that to Jeannie made his head look kind of like a mushroom.

"Neither Walter or Jeannie Morrell are anywhere to be found, and both seem to have made it away from here," he pleasantly reported, despite Clovis's demonic tone. "Based on the fact that one of our men had his head eaten to a pulp, and the hounds by the tree-line are equally tattered, I'd say this was likely the indigenous people of the North. That, or I suppose it is also possible that a smaller gang got hungry and ate most of this unfortunate soul's skull, as well as snacking on the dogs."

Jeannie furrowed her brow at the oddity of this fellow. Although what he said was utterly ridiculous, she found it strange that he didn't seem to utter it with the least bit of sarcasm.

"We found Walter's pin!" another man suddenly cheered.

"See, Clovis my friend?" Devin chirped. "Nothing to worry about. Our comrade will be found, and there's a possibility we'll be able to melt the skin off monstrous cannibals!"

Dominic sighed, suddenly, and whispered, "Children, I've seen enough. They'll be on the trail of Hanzah's people. We must stay out of sight and cross the river at our camp. We can head back toward Harran and plan our next move from there. I'd very much like to avoid these men. They are fiends like the rest, I'm sure, and they're still after you, Jeannie."

Jeannie sucked in a breath at the reminder but pulled her shoulders back to hide her fear. She nodded at Dominic, and the comrades crept away from their hiding place and back downstream toward their camp.

Once they were out of earshot from the Keagans, Jeannie gently sang a hymn her mother, Gwendolyn, once sang her called, "When the Shadows Run," as they quickly packed up their camp. Hanzah and Dominic turned to her in surprise when she began, but neither said anything to stop her as she sang:

When you sound the call, with spirit true,

I swear I'll hear that sound in you.

And when you run, with a head and a start,

From shadows that would break your heart,

My love you'll see my light shine through,

Those shadows chasing after you.

So even when the black night hums,

Still don't look back, the sun will come.

No don't look back, the sun will come.

Though Hanzah struggled to maintain any degree of positivity, he was beginning to appreciate Dominic's light-heartedness. After having crossed the river, he, Jeannie, and Dominic pressed through the forest back toward Harran. They moved quietly, as they figured there could be stragglers from the Keagan group.

Yet when the tension was at its highest, Dominic interrupted the silence and asked, "Would you both like to hear a joke?"

"Please," Hanzah answered, with a smile, relieved to ease even a bit of the tension.

"Well, have you both seen how geese fly in a 'V' formation?" he asked.

Hanzah nodded, and, out of the corner of his eye, he saw that Jeannie did, as well.

"Ok, so why do you think it is that one leg of the 'V' is always longer than the other?" Dominic continued.

"My people are connected to them, and still I do not know," Hanzah joked.

They were now within feet of the end of the forest.

"It's longer because that leg has more birds in . . . in it . . ." Dominic answered, his voice becoming distracted and trailing off the moment they emerged from the trees. Before them, the remains of the Morrell home stood, burned to the ground. Hanzah knew he wasn't imagining the sight when Jeannie suddenly reacted, simply crumbling to the ground. Hanzah rushed over and wrapped his arms around her, looking out at the rubble while she wailed with a sorrow that he could feel mirrored inside him.

He could not believe his eyes. Of all the disorder that the men of the East brought to the Territory, his father always told him that the Morrells would stand tall. Arkouda understood the value that Adonis and his family brought to the Riverlands, as well as the entirety of the North, and Hanzah feared for the fate of his home without these two great men. The thought also brought with it an epiphany. He was aware that the Keagans would certainly now be hunting his people, yet he struggled with the thought of helping the men who killed his father. The dangerous journey he would now have to make north into the Mountainlands was thanks to them. Sending word that he was alive through the birds would not be enough when the councilmen had surely sent contradictory messages. He knew he could never forgive them for what they did. But with his sister back at the camp, could he allow the Keagans to trail them without sending any warning? If his people were found, the retaliation would certainly be relentless. They had killed Keagan men and taken Walter Keagan himself. So Hanzah knew he had a decision to make.

Jeannie was now starting to calm, so the trio tentatively walked closer to what remained of her home. They found a place to sit among the rubble and take a moment of respect, a moment to recognize the sorrow and also let it pass.

After a few minutes Dominic asked, "My poor girl, if it's too much to ask, then please don't trouble yourself, but could you tell us what took place here? How did this happen?"

Hanzah watched Jeannie intently, wondering if she'd be able to tell the tale. He'd struggled to tell that of his father.

Jeannie wiped her eyes dry and began, "A few weeks ago a well-dressed man came into town saying he wanted to do business with our father. At the time I didn't know by his clothing or his pin that he was a Keagan. All I really noticed was his fancy dress and the speed of his horse." She cringed as she spoke of him. "He later came back, only this time he came to our home. He told us then that his name was Daniel Keagan. He discussed business with our father and told him that he ran a similar operation in the south with his brother William and was interested in a partnership of some kind. As much as I now hate this man, he was likeable, and my father was kind, so he spoke of our operations here and their scale. I didn't see it then," she said in despair, "but now when I look back on it I can remember the greed in his eyes. I remember how bright they became when he heard of my father's success. He was just too polite for me to recognize it at the time."

Hanzah knew firsthand it could be difficult to recognize the greed in any man's eyes—he hadn't seen it in Lennox's, confusing it for frustration or passion.

"Was this Daniel fellow the man who attacked your home?" Dominic asked.

"No," Jeannie said as she looked up at Dominic. "He left that night and never came back. The man who did come back was with those we saw at the river, and he was far worse. Though I didn't see his face at the time, he loudly introduced himself as Daniel's brother, Clovis Keagan. I only heard his voice, as I was in the back of the house then, but in every word I could hear a cold evil. My father spoke to him and tried to tell him that an agreement could be made, but he demanded my family leave town and give all we had to them. Everything my dad ever worked for."

She stopped for a moment, and Dominic placed his hand on her shoulder. "You can stop if you need to, my dear," he assured her.

Jeannie shook her head. "No, it's all right. My father told them that he'd surrender once he gathered my family. When he came back inside, he wore a look of despair I'd never seen before. It broke my heart, and for that alone, I wanted nothing more than to make them pay. That's when we all began to smell the smoke, but by then, it was too late. My mother had me escape out the back and run off into the woods. She told me my brothers were upstairs, so she and my father needed to try to save them. I suppose they just didn't want them to die alone. She told me how much she loved me, and off I went." Jeannie was once again in tears.

Hanzah approached her and wrapped an arm around her shoulder. They were bonded by their losses, and, because of that, he would hold it there for her as long as she needed.

Sometime after, Dominic gently said, "We can make camp here for a while. I don't expect them to return to this place. After we get some rest, we'll head to town to stop at my home. I have some last things to tend to and some supplies to retrieve—things we'll need. We'll discuss our next step then."

Hanzah nodded and, with a final squeeze of Jeannie's shoulder, he moved to begin setting up camp with Dominic. Once finished, Jeannie and Dominic soon fell asleep, but Hanzah lay in his spot wide awake. After contemplating his decision for a few minutes, he got up, walked toward the tree line, and took a knee. Hearing of the terror that occurred here had brought him to his decision. He could not knowingly let these treacherous Keagans reach his sister or his people and was determined to prevent it no matter who received his message. He hesitated again for only an instant, but reassured himself and called up to the wind. An eagle replied.

*

When the wedding day came, William was stressed. He had so many thoughts racing through his mind, although his most prevalent feeling was still one of happiness. When it was arranged for the Abigales to come to the Territory, he did not anticipate actually falling for Judith whatsoever. From what he had heard, she was a simple, proper lady, and though he placed great emphasis on being outwardly proper, it wasn't true to who he was on the inside. Now that the wedding day was here, and he knew the real Judith, he was so elated that he truly felt love for his bride.

While preparing for the ceremony, he was joined by Henry Abigale, Daniel, and the chauffeur, Cassius.

"You remind me very much of your father as a young man, William," Mr. Abigale said in admiration.

William turned his head slowly toward Mr. Abigale, his movement like that of an owl.

"If I turn out to be anything like my father as an older man then I'll remember that as an insult," William icily replied.

"Oh, I didn't mean anything negative by it I jus—," Mr. Abigale started.

"Henry please," William chuckled as a grin snapped across his face, and he loosened back up. "I was joking!"

"Oh, well, of course!" Mr. Abigale lightly replied. "He just had the same look of ambition that I see in you every day—that was all I meant anyway. Please excuse me now though, I have to prepare to walk your bride down the aisle and to appease Mrs. Abigale's every whim to ensure this affair meets her impossible standards," he praised with a wink. "I'll see you all out there!"

Once Henry left, Daniel walked up to his brother and dusted off his suit. "You ready, Billy?" he asked. At times, it was hard for even William to believe that Daniel was not the eldest of the Keagan brothers. Despite the fact that William was the leader here in the Murrieta, Daniel had always been the one who looked out for the other two. He was certainly the kindest and most well liked in any case.

"I'm about as ready as I ever could be," William replied, feeling somewhat awkward and nervous. He was as well-groomed as he'd been in his entire life, and though he appreciated appearance, he couldn't deny feeling somewhat uncomfortable with it. "This woman will be my queen with the help of her father."

"That she will, and you'll be king," Daniel encouraged him.

Suddenly, a knock came to the door, and Gregory entered the room. William thought that the giant man always looked odd in formal clothes. It was as if none could ever be made to fit him properly.

"Gregory, what can I do for you, my friend?" William asked.

"Sir, we've received news from Clovis of our exploits in the North," he replied.

Daniel turned to Cassius, "Thank you for your assistance, sir. You've been a tremendous help to our family, as well as the Abigales. If you could please go outside now and prepare for the ceremony while we discuss business, that'd be greatly appreciated."

Cassius acknowledged Daniel with a shake of his hand.

Matching Daniel's level of politeness, he chirped, "Of course. If you need anything at all, please don't hesitate to come find me. I'd be glad to accommodate any request that you may have. I'm here to serve the Abigales and now that will include serving you, as well."

William was beginning to warm up to this mysterious man and believed his skills could be utilized in some way if—or when—the time came. He intended to test his loyalty at a later time, however, and today was not that day. He then looked down and noticed that Cassius was still gripping Daniel's hand. Odd, that.

"Thanks again, Cassius. See you outside," Daniel replied smoothly, as Cassius nodded and finally relinquished his grip.

Once Cassius left the room, the Keagans' attention fixed onto Gregory.

"Clovis sent one of our men back from Harran. He says the town is under our control, but there was an issue with the Morrell family," Gregory said.

This news brought a sour taste to William's mouth. The Morrells were the key to controlling the North. "What kind of issue?" William asked slowly with a calm anger.

Gregory hesitated. "Billy," he started, "I'm sorry to be the one to tell you this, but Clovis's man said they weren't intimidated none. He said shots were fired from the home so . . . so Clovis had no choice but to defend the men. In the end, they burned the house to the ground with the Morrells inside it."

William looked at Gregory and then at Daniel in shock. "Why in the hell would they go shooting at a group of a hundred men?" William blurted.

"I suppose it could have been out of pride, or stupidity, or both,"

Daniel replied with a contemplative look on his face. "Maybe it was an accident?" he added.

"Psh! Daniel, come on. I expect better from you. You know accidents like that simply do not happen," William joked. "Whatever it was though, now we'll have to start from goddamn square one up there. Our hostile takeover plan was certainly an easier, more ideal one, so I suppose it was a nice try there, brother," he commended Daniel who beamed at him.

"Perhaps we won't have to change our strategy at all though, Billy," Gregory added. "I didn't get to finish the rest of the details of the incident. The man also said that one of the members of the family survived. It was the daughter, Jeannie Morrell. Unfortunately she escaped, but she's believed to be alive."

William looked up, excitement filling him, but Daniel responded first, "This is great news, we must find her! She'll still have the trust of the people in the North and, with some convincing, can allow us to fill the void."

"Yes, though unfortunately it won't be easy," Gregory said. "Clovis sent Walter and a group of men into the woods after her, and they were met by the V'ahani clan. All the bodies were located except Walter's and Jeannie's. The last the messenger heard was that Clovis believes Walter is being held captive and that the girl is likely with them, as well."

"Good lord, Gregory, you're just lifting me up and throwing me back to the cold ground right now aren't you? So what now?" William asked.

"What do you mean, Billy?" Gregory followed.

"Did he not say what the lowly tribesmen intend to do next?"

William asked again with great anticipation.

"Oh yes, Clovis believes they're now headed south. He said that he'll stalk them and get back Walter and the girl," Gregory finished.

Daniel looked at William and reported, "Overall this is great news. Not exactly according to plan, but nothing ever is."

"Very true," William agreed, feeling himself calm. "I must ask you to travel to Harran now, Daniel. After the wedding, of course. I'll send you with a contingent of men who'll assist you in holding the town. I need you to begin establishing our trade relationships in the Riverlands. Once the girl's located, I want there to be a seamless transition, so that we have a hand in all dealings from that point through the south. When that's complete, it'll just be a matter of taking the diamond-rich Mountainlands and their Fortress."

"I'll gladly go and work my magic, Billy!" Daniel exclaimed. "Now let's go out there and get you married!"

As they filed out of the room, they noticed Cassius walking away. William thought it odd, but he was looking forward to the wedding too much to dwell on it.

That winter day couldn't have been more beautiful, nor the decoration more elegant outside of the Keagan mansion. William marveled that people from all over Fayette were in attendance, all clamoring to witness what would be a marriage of the most powerful people in the Murrieta. Almost all of the men and women originated in the East, so they all would know the influence of both the Keagan and Abigale families. Both families sat in the front. Blanton and Donna sat next to Francis, Florence, and Henrietta. By now, it seemed Francis's experience with the Keagan twins had taught him not to question them. In fact, the children were all beginning to become somewhat friendly. Florence and Henrietta even played with Donna on occasion, though Blanton still always needed to be present, much to his dismay. Clovis and Walter were in their predicament and therefore absent, but otherwise all was going well.

William could not wait to see his bride. He was so excited to have an equally ambitious companion with whom he could share his dreams and power. It certainly didn't hurt either that she was an incredibly beautiful young woman or that she brought with her even greater opportunity than he was already seizing here in the Murrieta. Unable to wait, he came to the kitchen where she was making last-minute preparations with her mother and father.

William could tell Judith was rather stressed, so he remained quiet after greeting Henry. Maria offered Judith a glass of wine.

"Here, honey, take a sip of this," she said. "It's imported, and it's delicious. It'll calm your nerves."

While looking out at the altar, Judith hurriedly reached for the glass. Still staring at the scene outside, she moved the glass quickly and clumsily toward her mouth. Her carelessness caused her to spill some of the drink down the side of her face and onto her neck.

"SHIT!! Get me a damn wash cloth please!" she blurted, wiping her face with one hand and preventing the wine from reaching her dress with the other. She was successful in this maneuver, but the stream of red wine now stained her neck.

William suppressed a chuckle. It oddly pleased him to see her as nervous as he felt.

Maria hurried over to Judith with the cloth. "Please don't use that language in front of your parents!" she pleaded. "Don't lose your head, everything's going to be okay, my love," she added as she wiped Judith's neck clean. "When your father and I got married, I didn't have my mother to re-assure me. Not because she wasn't alive at the time, but because she had drank completely too much wine and was out-of-her-mind drunk. She even had to be escorted back to her room by my father, who she blamed for the whole thing, and missed the whole ceremony!" They laughed together at this. "I was extremely embarrassed at the time, but the night belonged to your father and I, and nothing could take that away from us. You'll find the same is the case for you no matter what happens, I promise."

William was glad this reassurance seemed to calm his bride, for with a deep breath, she told her mother she was ready. William quietly exited and went to take his place by the altar.

The ceremony went on without a hitch. It was exactly as William had hoped and how he promised Judith it would go. Once it was over, those in attendance gathered in the reception area. The food and wine were delicious, as advertised, and everyone was having a great time. William was certainly one of the happiest men in the Murrieta and was very much enjoying the wine himself.

The more he drank, the more talkative he became, and after a few hours he had spoken to nearly everyone in attendance. He later found his way over to Daniel. "This is really happening, my brother," he said in a somewhat slurred voice.

"Yes, this is all real," Daniel said as he put his arm around William's shoulder with a laugh.

William steadied himself and clarified, "No, I mean our success here. It is really happening."

"Yes, that is real, too. It is extremely impressive what you've been able to accomplish, Billy," he lauded.

William looked at his brother with bloodshot eyes and a face lit up by the praise. "Do you think father will approve of us now? Do you think he will respect us as equals again?" he asked hopefully.

"I wish I could say with certainty, but there is no telling with him," Daniel replied with a sigh as he looked out to the open field of the mansion yard. "But, you shouldn't worry yourself if he doesn't, Billy. You've achieved so much. His approval is too unreliable a thing for earning it to be your only goal."

This troubled William, though it was not the first time Daniel tried to tell him this. He looked down at the ground with despair. No matter what Daniel said, his desire to gain his father's approval was unflappable. It drove him like nothing else. He began thinking of the possibility of never getting to that point, and it started to cause a sharp pain behind his eyes.

"I don't feel well," William told his brother as he began to clench his head.

Daniel held him up slightly as he began to sway.

"Let's get you inside to relax for a little while," he said.

In that moment though, William's pain intensified, and he started to groan under his breath. Daniel became more insistent on getting him inside before anyone noticed. William then looked out onto the field. On the horizon in the far distance he saw a blurry figure in white standing completely still. To him it looked to be about the height of a child.

"What is that?" he asked pointing in that direction. Sweat was now profusely dripping down from his face.

Daniel looked puzzled. "There's nothing there, Billy. Come on, let's go."

Suddenly, the sky started to darken, and worried voices filled the reception room. William looked up to see the largest mass of crows he had ever seen.

". . . in the hell?" Daniel said quietly, assuring William that this time he wasn't the only one seeing the phenomenon.

Then the sound hit them.

The noise the crows emitted as they flew above them was as massive as the flock itself, which completely filled the sky. Guests began to panic as the crows blocked out the sun, leaving the entire setting in darkness. Food and drinks were knocked to the floor, and glassware was shattered. All in attendance stared up in disbelief. But William didn't feel shock so much as a foreboding.

"They flew in from the North," William had to yell, leaning towards Daniel. "What does it mean?" he shouted again.

Of course, no answer came.

A few minutes later, the last of the crows passed, and the fly-over ended.

Daniel turned to William and shakily said, "Find your wife and get inside. I'll calm the guests and see them out. We'll figure this out once we've ensured this wedding has ended on a positive note."

William nodded, and then found and held his wife, leading her inside. He left Daniel to the work of charming each and every guest as he'd promised.

CHAPTER 4

FIRST JT GIVETH

Dominic sat quietly, making last minute preparations in his mind. The sun had risen, and it was time for him, Jeannie, and Hanzah to continue into Harran, which was now inhabited by a contingent of the Keagan Gang. These men were certainly all aware that Jeannie was on the loose, and the sight of a V'ahani in Harran alone would be suspicious. Dominic knew that they'd have to be swift if they were to make it to his home unseen. He had spent the entire night drawing up plans to sneak the children in and felt that he had several ideas with potential.

He signaled to Hanzah, and after they had finished gathering the supplies, Dominic gently approached Jeannie, who sat in what was likely once her front yard with her hands around her knees.

"I'm afraid it's time to go, Jeannie," Dominic said apologetically. He felt for the girl's pain and hated to have the burden of being the one to constantly point out reality to her.

To his surprise and relief she graciously replied. "I know. I'm ready."

Hanzah then helped her to her feet, and their march began.

Dominic opted to describe his intentions to the children as they made their way toward the town. "During the day, the Keagans will likely be scattered about town," he started. "Our chance to sneak you children in will come at night, at which point most of them will probably be at the saloon. The town is small, so there shouldn't be too many inhabiting it, and for out-of-towners, the saloon is one of the only sources of entertainment. Once we reach the outskirts of Harran, you'll remain there in hiding through the day while I drop Nala and my supplies off at my home. I'll also scout out how many of them there are. Then, when the night comes, I'll go to the saloon to ensure they are distracted. Once they are, I'll make my exit and give you both a signal. That's when we'll hurry you along in the shadows to my home. I know that was a lot, but any questions?"

"Yes, where will we hide while you distract them?" Hanzah asked.

"The saloon will be one of the first buildings you'll see when we reach the town, so you'll be in the same hiding place you start in," Dominic answered. "When the time comes, I'll whistle two times as such." He let out a whistle like a birdcall. "Then you'll meet me in the back of the hotel which sits next to the saloon, and we'll go from there."

"So we are just to sit there all day helplessly? What if we end up found?" Hanzah worried.

"Also, will the trip out of town not be even more difficult than the trip into it?" Jeannie added inquisitively.

"I understand your fears. I have my own as well. But if we don't make this stop now, I'm afraid we don't currently have the resources to reach our next destination at all, wherever that may be," Dominic replied somberly as they walked, "And to answer your question, Jeannie, no, leaving town should be much simpler.

An illusionist always has a trick up his sleeve. Unfortunately, at the moment the shirt with the sleeve I need is in my home!" This part was true, though he neglected to mention that the illusion itself would be tricky. No need to make the kids more nervous than they already were.

After a short time, they began approaching the town. Before setting the young ones up in their hiding place, Dominic tied up Nala. He then crept with them to a swath of high bushes that were thick enough to conceal them. As promised, from a distance they could see the town and location of the saloon.

"All right friends, this is where I must leave you for now," Dominic whispered. "Remember to stay alert for my signal and remain hidden. I'll see you again shortly." He reverted back up the trail to retrieve his horse and then continued again into town. Though he was usually not one to worry, he knew he would have to calm his nerves as he'd done many times before in preparation for his shows.

By the time Dominic reached his home, put Nala in the stable, gathered all the supplies he would need for a long journey, and prepared a space for the children to sleep, hours had passed, and the sun was just beginning to set. While walking through town, he also noticed that there could not have been more than twenty Keagan men total in all of Harran. Based on the personalities he saw, he also figured his odds would be fairly strong of the saloon being full. When he arrived, this thought was confirmed. Though he didn't get an exact count, it appeared that at the very least, a large portion of the people residing in Harran were drinking merrily on this night. His plan was to assist them in drinking themselves into a stupor so that the children and he could move around more easily and remain undetected.

Luckily, they were already making this quite easy for him on their own. It only helped that most of the beautiful young women residing in Harran also filled the saloon that evening. Clearly, the girls were doing their part to keep the Keagan men occupied. Upon entering, Dominic headed straight for the bar, avoiding the occupied tables. Sitting alone, he ordered a pint of beer as he watched the Keagan men gracelessly attempt to court the ladies of Harran. He noted, too, that the regular male inhabitants of the town sat quietly, seeming too nervous to intrude on the Keagans' prowling. Soon enough a boisterous young man came and sat next to him.

"Who are you, fancy boy?" the man asked loudly.

Dominic smiled, ever polite but naturally impatient with the socially inept, "Hello there, my name is Nicholas Macfarlane. What's your name, friend?" he greeted, unable to decide whether the fellow's manners or abnormally thick moustache was more obnoxious.

"Right, then," the man replied mockingly, "I'm Jesse, good sir. Jesse Billings."

Dominic could tell this Jesse was amused with himself.

"Well, Jesse Billings, how about I treat you and your friends to a drink? As a welcome to my fair town," he declared.

Jesse laughed, "Let's be careful about calling this 'your' town anymore, but I couldn't turn down a drink. Especially not when these fellas are offered one, as well."

He then shouted the offer to the Keagans in the room, and, just like that, Dominic was in. News of his illusionist profession skipped from seat to seat like a pebble thrown on the water, and before he knew it, he was doing tricks for the enemy. This was something he had actually prepared for, though he did not expect for things to go so smoothly. As the night went on, the men became more and more drunk. They sang songs, they spilled glasses, and they cheered to their successes. Several also began looking at Dominic with awe and loudly debated with each other where he and his "magical powers" originated. One thing Dominic always loved about his profession was the wonder it inspired in those of all ages.

Once it seemed like they were beginning to forget their own names, he decided it was time to leave. "Well friends, I must be going," he informed them. "I'll be leaving in the morning to do a performance a bit further west so I need to get my sleep."

Jesse looked up with glazed, bloodshot eyes. "Oh no!" he called out in his slurred, drunken voice. "Daniel jus' got to town this morning an' he would've loved to see some tricks."

Dominic's heart sank as he discovered the news that a Keagan brother was in town—especially since this brother had seen Jeannie firsthand. "Oh?" Dominic asked under his breath. "Why didn't he join us in the saloon tonight?"

"He's sleepin' I b'lieve. He had a long day travelin' in an' such. He'll want to meet you t'morrow though fer shur," Jesse told him with as stern a look as a drunken man could have.

Dominic looked down and lied, "Well, I'll definitely make a point to meet him tomorrow before I go then. You all have yourselves a good night."

"You, too, Nick'las," Jesse belched.

Dominic's sense of urgency to get his comrades out of town as soon as possible had dramatically increased with this news. There was no time to waste. He exited the saloon, jogged to the planned meeting place behind the hotel, and when the coast seemed clear, whistled out to the children. Jeannie and Hanzah came running down to him. They both seemed thrilled to finally be able to leave the spot where they had been crouched for most of the day.

When they got to him he whispered, "We must be quick now."

They nodded, he turned, and they all moved around the side of the hotel in the direction of Dominic's house. As they rounded the corner, however, they heard two men greet each other very briefly. Dominic held up a hand, and they all froze in their tracks, but he had little time to react beyond that as Jesse Billings suddenly appeared.

Dominic hastily scanned the streets behind Jesse to see if anyone else was behind him. There was no one.

Confused and drunk, Jesse asked, "Nick'las, who're yer little friends?"

Dominic stammered at first but found a way to put together a response.

"Uh, these are my assistants. Obviously they're not quite of the age to appreciate a drink, so they didn't join me at the saloon. We were just on our way back to my home and must be going."

"HOLD UP!" the man shouted in excitement. "These chil'ren are magic too!? Show me a trick chil'ren!"

"It's really too late for them, so we need to head home. They're quite tired, I'm afraid," Dominic pleaded.

"Nonsense!" Jesse declared. "There's surely time for one trick! Please."

Dominic rolled his eyes. "Okay," he sulked. "Um. Okay, I have one." Motioning to Jeannie he asked, "All right, my dear, please go stand by the wall of the hotel with your arms and legs outstretched like a star." She looked at him in disbelief but he nudged her forward. "I have two throwing knives and that's all I have time for, sir," he noted, looking to Jesse who nodded with the excitement of a young child.

Fortunately for Jeannie, Dominic was a very skilled knife thrower. So many times before others needed to trust in his abilities, and his confidence was no issue at his shows. However, his shows were during the daytime or with the benefit of light, and he only prayed she would not move in the darkness.

"Be very still now, my dear," he said as he lifted the knife. "Breathe deeply and don't move a muscle. When I count down from three, I will throw. Ready?" The tension among the four was growing as they stood just off the otherwise silent street. He began, "Three . . ." and without warning he immediately threw the knife, which landed just between Jeannie's head and right shoulder. She stood shaking, but he knew the best way would be to get through it rapidly.

Jesse stood next to him, mouth and eyes wide. "Well shit! That was brilliant," he declared. "Again!"

This time, Dominic was the one who took a deep breath. On the next throw he gave her a full countdown and hurled the second throwing knife. This one landed just between Jeannie's left arm and leg. The illusionist was overcome with relief as Jeannie began to move away from the wall.

Dominic turned to Jesse and chirped, "Hope you enjoyed the

show and have a good rest of your night, sir. Now, we must be off."

The drunken man lost all childish excitement that he previously had. In a dark, cold tone he uttered, "No." Though he was certainly still drunk, his voice no longer sounded it in that moment. He reached for a hunting knife that had been attached to his waist, extended it to Dominic, and demanded, "One more."

Dominic stared at Jesse with a challenging glance, while Jeannie continued to shake in terror. His distaste for this man had been building since the moment he met him, and he was just ready to be done with him.

"Please, Jesse," he replied, "Please don't make me do this. It's too dark outside, and we're all tired."

"I don't think it's too much to ask," Jesse demanded. "And like I said, this isn't your town anymore. You need to learn that you don't get to choose. We choose now. And I say you're throwing that damn knife."

Dominic let out a deep, downward breath. "Okay, Jesse," he sighed.

He gestured for Jeannie to go back to the wall. She and Hanzah both looked at him in disbelief, while Jesse's expression had returned to its original giddiness.

"Let's see it then!" he cheered.

Dominic looked into Jeannie's eyes and promised, "My dear, this will all be over shortly."

He then hoisted up the heavy knife to aim. He took a minute to analyze. "You know Jesse, this knife is obviously heavier than the ones I threw before, which will make it even more miraculous when I hit my target," he smoothly explained as he took aim. "I take it you're perfectly aware of that though."

Jesse's gaze was still set on Jeannie as he laughed and replied, "I might very well be aware of that. We'll be seein' what you're made of tonight!"

"Yes, we will," Dominic replied. His hands were now sweating, and he was horribly worried. "You know, I hope you've enjoyed my town, Jesse, though I wish you had never come to it."

Jesse began to turn his head towards Dominic just as the illusionist heaved the hunting knife, which landed right between the drunken man's eyes.

Jesse fell straight to the ground. Dominic, breathing heavily, thought how it never became any easier to kill a man, even if one knew how to do it and had done it before. Killing was something he hoped he would never have to do again, but at this moment, he couldn't think, he needed to act.

He looked urgently toward the unmoving Jeannie and Hanzah and whispered, "There's no time to be afraid, my friends. We need to hide his body right now!"

Dominic desperately wrapped his jacket around Jesse's face to keep the blood from leaving a trail. Together they then lifted the corpse and hurriedly maneuvered it through the streets to Dominic's home.

Later that night, he alone would bury it, breathing and sweating heavily while he periodically cracked his knuckles in a fury. As much as he did feel relief that no one would ever have to be bothered by Jesse Billings again, he still wished it hadn't come to taking the man's life. What if there could have been another way? Had he thought it through enough? Had he been wrong? Before he knew it, he was brought back to the darkest time of his life—to a place he'd hoped for so long that he would never visit again.

*

As the V'ahani pressed on, Latera was beginning to notice an uneasiness in the councilmen. Lennox, for one, was constantly looking over his shoulder, as if he were preparing for anything and everything that might interrupt them. Parish acted similarly, however, he seemed a little less fidgety than the Chieftain. Lastly, there was Castor. The final councilman seemed to her to be taking the loss of his leader and friend the hardest. Plodding along on horseback, he began to ramble to no person in particular. Latera certainly felt for the plight of the councilmen, not only in their loss, but also, in their stress, about the decision they had made for their people. As time went on, she more and more wanted to support them—to support the entire group.

"The wind is too quiet," she heard Castor say in a shaky tone, running his hands through his beard. They had now cleared the forest of the Riverlands and were heading towards the hilly, open terrain of the central Murrieta. "It is far too quiet. The Mother speaks with her silence and we are in danger. Yes, yes, in grave danger. I am certain of it."

"Collect yourself, Castor," Lennox grumpily replied. "We must show confidence for our people if we are to guide them south."

"Yes, yes, I am confident of it. Indeed," Castor answered with a deep sigh.

"We have to be sure his mouth stays shut, so his lunacy does not discourage anyone," Parish whispered to Lennox. He did not speak nearly quietly enough for anyone around him not to hear, but Latera could tell it didn't matter to the man, who seemed wholly preoccupied. "If he breaks their spirit, this will have all been for nothing," he finished.

"He will not say anything that would put us in jeopardy," Lennox replied. "Even if he did, his words would hardly be coherent."

The councilmen did not speak again for some time as they continued on, but Latera wondered what Lennox meant about placing them in jeopardy. Perhaps he spoke of their people. Latera certainly agreed that doubt could place their people in jeopardy on this perilous journey, and she turned her attention to the rest of the clan.

The V'ahani were still doing well on supplies and, with the help of Elan, Latera worked continuously to keep morale high. The two were inseparable since the trip began, and she was pleased with how supportive he was being of her efforts.

"You do not have to do all this you know," she said appreciatively as they rode alongside one another. He had just regrouped with her after fetching water for some of those marching. "It is very kind of you, but you are already a hero for making this journey."

He looked pleased that she called him that. She had a feeling that was the word he'd always longed to be called.

"I know I do not have to," he replied gallantly. "I did not have to be the one to make the journey north either, but I chose to and I also choose to help you . . . and your people."

"Well you should know I am very thankful for that," she said as she blushed, noticing his slip-up.

They continued to walk on, and soon they approached the top

of the long, rocky field they trekked along. When they did, Elan's eyes widened. He then hurried his horse on toward it.

"Where is he off to?!" shouted Lennox.

At the top, Elan halted his steed.

When the others caught up, he explained, "This is the campsite I departed from not long ago before I found you all. It is the last place I saw my people. These were our camp grounds."

The V'ahani looked out in shock.

"Do you see what they have done to the native homes?" Lennox called out to his people in a rallying rage as he stared down at the chained Walter Keagan, who was hunched over an only mildly sturdy tree branch, which he had been given to maintain his balance on his wounded leg. Walter spit vilely on the ground in Lennox's direction in response. "They have defiled a people who are not so different from ourselves. The Territory is OUR home. It is not for them to exploit and destroy!" The V'ahani cheered out in unison. "We will settle here tonight and rebuild this camp in memory of those who were here before. This place shall stand again from the ashes before we continue on!"

When they reached the camp, the entire group contributed to the rebuilding effort. In no time at all, the evening came, but with all their efforts, they completed the task.

The V'ahani then retreated to their designated shelters. Inside her tent, Latera prepared for sleep. As much as she missed her father and brother, she was very pleased with the progress that her people had made thus far. It was a testament to the strength her father had instilled in them.

As she lay in her cot, there was a whisper from outside.

"Latera, are you awake?" It was Elan.

She was glad he was there, and she came to the entrance and replied, "For now, I was about to get to sleep. Is everything all right?"

"Yes, everything is fine," he said. "I was just thinking of you out here and was standing around being timid about coming to talk to you." She giggled at him and he laughed with her. "I am not used to the cold like you are though, so I was hoping I could come in before I freeze myself."

She laughed again, "Well we would not want that! Of course, Elan, come inside."

He thanked her and walked in behind her. "Lennox's words were very kind. I am very thankful to see this camp restored," he said.

"Yes, that was kind of him," she replied. "Are you thirsty, by the way? You have been giving water out all day, so I was not sure if you had any yourself!"

"Yes, I am actually rather thirsty," he answered jauntily.

She got water for each of them and sat down by her cot. After they took a swig, he gestured if he could sit with her, and she nodded her assent.

"Can I ask you something, Latera?"

"Of course," she replied.

He hesitated at first, but then began, "I only saw your father two times. The first time, he held a blade to my throat and threatened my life." By now they were both able to laugh together at that recollection, which they did, and then he continued. "The second time was in my cell, and then I never saw him after that, as you know. And I am so sorry for that loss, Latera. I am so sorry those monsters got to him." He paused, sincerity filling his expression. With all the upheaval and chaos in the move to the south, she felt like he'd been one of the first people to truly give his condolences to her in such a genuine way, and she was grateful to him for it. "During that second encounter though," he continued, "I saw something truly remarkable in him. He was the only man in the room to exhibit this, as well, which shows how rare it can be. It was his patience. He had the innate ability to know that what may not seem like the right decision immediately might ultimately be exactly the thing that is needed in the long run. Though my people do not have Chieftains and councilmen, I hope one day I can be a leader like him. So, my question is whether you could simply tell me more about him?"

As she was listening, her mind played back the memories of her father and of how he exhibited exactly the trait Elan described. At first she felt only joy, but she became more upset as she worried that her father's patience in the decision to make the journey south might have ultimately been what led to his demise.

"Patience was one thing he certainly did have," she recalled as she was overcome with emotion.

"Oh no, I am sorry I brought it up. Are you okay?" he asked, moving closer to her side.

"Yeah, I will be all right," she replied. "I just miss them."

"And I am sure that you always will," Elan said. "I cannot imagine what you must be going through, but I promise you that we will make this unification happen in his honor and all of the Murrieta will be better for it. All of its people will be brought together, and we will build a place together that he would be proud of!"

Latera smiled. She enjoyed his enthusiasm and hoped he was right.

"Elan, thank you for coming to talk to me," she offered. "I needed this, and I am really glad I have you here to help my people and me through this." She leaned over to him and gave him a kiss on his cheek, to which he blushed and grinned ear to ear. "I think I should be getting some rest now, but I will talk to you more in the morning?" she asked.

"You most certainly will! Goodnight!" Elan cheered like he had achieved a victory.

Latera giggled at his stumble as he exited her tent. As she laid her head down and closed her eyes, a smile lit her face and remained there through the night.

*

After the body was buried and the children were asleep, Dominic headed to the home of Charles Langston. Dominic, like most who knew Charles, thought him to be mostly odd and dimwitted. However, if there was anything useful in the man's head, it was his knowledge of all things Harran. He would be the only one who could clue Dominic in to the plans of the Keagans in the North. Though Charles could be a useful tool, Dominic knew he had to be careful with his words. The, self-proclaimed "mayor of Harran," was mostly friendly with him, but he understood that the gravity of the situation would make saying the right things crucial. This was especially the case when dealing with a person as simple as Charles.

Dominic knocked on the door and was startled when it was answered just seconds after doing so. It was almost as if Charles was simply standing behind the door, waiting for someone to knock. Dominic wondered whom this man could possibly be waiting for. Charles said nothing but stood looking at him with an anxious stare. Dominic could not help but think of how oddly shaped this man's balding head and body were. The comparison to a potato came to mind.

"Hello there, Charles," Dominic greeted with as much warmth as he could muster given the circumstances. After a pause, Charles still said nothing. "I was hoping I could come in and have a word with you. Maybe we could catch up. It's been a while!" he continued.

Charles's expression finally filled with some form of animation. "It has," he replied. "Come inside."

Dominic walked in, and Charles gestured for them to sit at the dinner table. It was certainly a large table for someone who lived alone and had as few guests as Charles, Dominic thought. They awkwardly sat down at opposite ends of the table. Luckily for Charles, he did not seem socially aware enough to understand awkwardness and the pain Dominic would have to endure conversing in such a manner.

"So, the reason I came here is I went to the saloon tonight and heard some things from the men who were there. Things I thought you might be able to confirm for me," Dominic started.

"I may or may not be able to give you the information you're looking for," he said, crossing his hands and leaning back in his seat. "What did you hear?"

Dominic chose his next words carefully as he replied, "Well, I was drinking with some Keagan men, and they mentioned that Daniel Keagan is in town. I was hoping you could tell me if this is true and what the implications will be on Harran as you see them." He thought asking Charles's own opinion on the matter would appease his ego and distract him.

"This is true," Charles confirmed matter-of-factly, as if to reveal some secret that only he was entrusted with. "Daniel is staying at the hotel next to the saloon. He arrived earlier today, and I spoke to him. He's a very kind, very intelligent man. He explained to me his sorrow when he heard what happened to the Morrells and apologized on behalf of the entire Keagan Gang. It's so unfortunate that the Morrells would be as stubborn as to shoot at all those men rather than just giving up."

This confused Dominic. "What do you mean 'shoot at' them?" he asked.

"Well, Daniel explained how he sent his brother Clovis with a group of men to demand the Morrells give up control of their business here. Hostile takeover kind of thing," he said. "The Keagans wanted the Morrells to essentially be their employees. They didn't intend to kill them at all, but Adonis forced their hand by firing upon them when Clovis arrived."

Once again Dominic reminded himself to speak carefully, though he struggled to do so. He wanted to explain to Charles the real story, but the man seemed infatuated by Daniel's allure.

"So what's next then for our home?" Dominic asked. "Are we to simply accept their control?"

"Of course we'll accept them," Charles declared. "I trust Daniel Keagan. He told me I'll retain my title as mayor of Harran, and his family will only help us to grow. You shouldn't hide things from them either, Dominic. Those Kennedale sisters are doing just that—I'm sure of it. I don't know what yet, but I don't trust them, and they'll be exposed. You should go speak to Daniel, and you'll understand all that they have planned to help us."

Dominic could tell the conversation was over. The futility of talking to Charles any further had become clear. He sat in his chair contemplating for a few seconds and then lifted his head toward his host with the same fake grin he had when he entered.

"I appreciate your advice and will take it into consideration, Charles. I must be off now. It's been a long night. All the best to you, Mr. Mayor," he said as he stood up to leave.

"Please do more than consider it," Charles implored as he followed Dominic all the way out the door.

It was now getting late, and Dominic was exhausted as he parted from Charles's house. On the way back to his own home, he heard yelling. He recognized the high pitch screaming of the Kennedale sisters and began trotting toward the noise. As he got closer, he could make out what they were saying.

"You give me back my money, you vile bitch!" He heard a deep voice yell.

"You wanted to know your fortune, you agreed to pay!" Debra screeched back. "Ah! Let me go!"

Dominic heard a thud and hastened his pace toward the scuffle.

"I shouldn't have to pay y'all a god damn cent for your lies!"

Another thud came.

"Let her go, you asshole!" Cassie wailed. "You don't get to choose your fortune!"

"Oh I beg to differ, wench!" the man called out. "I'm about to choose y'alls fortunes that's for damn sure!"

A third thud came, followed by a scream from Cassie.

The yelling stopped for a few seconds, and then only moaning could be heard.

"You better not come back here, you piece of shit!" Cassie cried out.

As Dominic finally ran onto the scene, the man was gone, and Cassie was crouched over Debra, who was beaten badly.

"What happened here?" Dominic asked a sobbing Cassie.

"That Keagan good-for-nothing just beat my sister, because he didn't like his fortune, that's what happened!"

Dominic knew the Kennedale sisters well, and behind their rough exteriors, they were some of the most loyal friends he had met in his travels.

He helped Cassie bring Debra inside and tend to her wounds. After they bandaged her up they sat down together.

"How are you feeling?" he asked.

"Much better, thank you, Dominic," she replied.

Cassie added, "Yeah, we can't thank you enough, Dominic. Those brutes are ruining our town, and we just got sick of it. If there's anything at all we can do for you though, please just ask."

An epiphany then came to him. "Actually, there is something you can do," he said. "This evening I spoke to Charles Langston."

"That piece of shit," Cassie interrupted.

"I can understand why you'd say that," Dominic chuckled. "I'm afraid, as you seem to know, that he has a soft spot in is heart for the Keagans. He believes the town will be better off with them in place."

"Like I said," Cassie nodded, "piece of shit."

"Yes, well it seems his allegiance to them has brought him to a point of distrusting certain members of our community," he added. "In fact, Charles seems to believe that you sisters have a secret of some kind."

Dominic noticed that the eyes of the Kennedale sisters grew wide in response. They looked at each other and back at him. He was shocked that Charles's suspicions might actually be founded.

Leaning forward, he whispered to them with urgency, "What are you hiding?"

*

The sun was just beginning to show its first rays behind the hills. It kissed the rocky peaks as it rose with a sky behind it that was all shades of red and blue. Latera stood outside the campgrounds, scanning the surrounding area and admiring its warmth. She breathed in the scenery, which nourished her with the freshest of air. The crisp, earthy scent that she inhaled felt like home, yet she knew this place was unfamiliar. Now that she had a taste of adventure, there would be no going back. She had no one to go back to, in any case.

For some time, she soaked it all in, but her peace was soon interrupted by a faint calling. At first, she mistook it for a distant breeze, but it eventually became more distinct. Latera then recognized the noise in the air and looked up to the sky. A lone eagle revealed itself through the beams of sunshine.

"To whom do I speak?" It hissed to her in her native tongue as it glided overhead.

This question was curious, as whoever sent it must have been sending a tailored message. She wondered why and who it could be.

"I am Latera, of the V'ahani of the Riverlands," she declared.

The bird screeched in response as it circled overhead. With each fly by, a new phrase was uttered. "Latera," it icily whispered next, "this is Hanzah."

All the warmth that she had felt inside her just seconds ago suddenly vanished as her heart sank. Latera could not speak. She could not think. A part of her wondered if this could be real.

"You must remain calm, but I am alive," it called on its next pass.

Hanzah—alive! She began to choke up. It was real. Her brother lived.

"Our father, it was not the Keagans. The councilmen killed him, and I escaped."

Each new revelation spiked so many emotions inside her that she hardly knew what to feel anymore, but horror and rage were now rushing to the forefront. They had betrayed her father.

"I beg you, sister, you must remain calm. You must guide our people and be brave for them while I go north to inform Uncle Orrin of the truth. Our father was not killed by the Keagans, but I have seen them. They are dangerous and they are coming for you all. May we meet again, sister." With that the majestic bird flew off.

As soon as it cleared the hills, Latera began processing what she had just heard. Despite Hanzah's plea for calmness, there was a fury inside her that she could not ignore. Right then, she sprinted back toward the camp like a tiger toward its prey.

The morning sun had now risen fully into the sky, revealing

the campgrounds, but Latera's charge began to slowly subside as she became distracted: a noisy shape was swiftly covering any semblance of light. When she came to a complete stop, she looked up to see a tremendous mass of crows flying in overhead, whose shadow began to blanket the field in darkness.

From a distance, she could see the V'ahani beginning to emerge from their shelters. Along with the rest of them, Latera listened in to the hissing, which was coming from every direction. Voices from thousands of V'ahani of the Great Fortress travelled together bringing messages through the crows that she could make out in pieces. From the Grand Chieftain and his Masters, she was pleased to hear words of disfavor toward the new Chieftain and councilmen of the Riverlands for deciding to travel south without first consulting them. She lowered her eyes from the crows and looked to her people. She first spotted Elan among the crowd, who looked about as giddy as an occupied infant. It pleased her that he was being brought further into their world, and she noticed how genuine his intrigue was.

Then she was filled with pride as she looked upon the rest of her people and heard the messages sent for them. They all looked up in awe at the darkness and the sound that it created, receiving messages of encouragement. Many voices from the Mountainlands camps cheered for happiness at the prospect of peace. Her people were told to continue on safely and with bravery, as they would be defining the future of the V'ahani.

As she saw the confidence and joy this instilled in them, Latera now understood the importance of Hanzah's message of calmness. She felt proud that at his age he could be so brave and was pleased he learned so much from their father. In this moment, she realized that it was time for her to become the leader she knew she could be for her people. The one they currently lacked in their traitorous councilmen. She looked back on the councilmen with disgust as she could now recognize their erratic behavior as guilt. The negative messages certainly were not helping, either, and now they just seemed like outcasts. There would be a time for justice, she realized. And she would certainly need that time for her own satisfaction. But for now though, they were the least important people at the camp.

Then, among all the wonder, a scream rang out, followed by a thunderous pattering of hooves. From inside the darkness created by the birds, the sight of a battalion of men on horseback could just be made out. They charged full force at the camp from over the hill, several armed with torches.

In response, Latera ran to close the remaining distance to the camp and screamed at the top of her lungs, "Prepare for attack!"

Yet, it was too late for a significant defensive response as the men were nearly upon them now.

With the sound of the men and horses, the crows broke into a frenzy. The mass of birds descended on the camp almost simultaneously with the attacking mob. When the forces met at the campgrounds, it was a scene of havoc. Crows filled the air, colliding with horses, people, and other objects. All visibility was lost, as they flew in every direction. Indistinguishable screams rang out throughout the area.

Outside, Latera dodged left and right as all manner of crows, horses, and men whizzed past her. She could just make out through the birds that multiple tents had been lit ablaze. While distracted by the fires, she failed to recognize a horse barreling toward her. Just as she prepared for impact, however, she was suddenly snatched and pulled inside a nearby tent. Looking up she realized her rescuer was Elan, who was now crouched over her, shielding her with his body.

"Elan, you saved me! Thank you!" She shouted as she went to hug him.

Before she could reach him, he backed away, shaking. His eyes grew wide, and his face paled. "I only did what—what was necessary. Anyone would have done the same."

Latera was so confused by his response and the coldness that accompanied that she stared at him crookedly for a few seconds before her worry for her people took over, causing her to turn away from him. Peering through the tent she could see that as the fires grew, the birds began to disperse from the flames. Sounds and sights slowly became more recognizable. A few people who had been injured by the horses could be seen on the ground screaming in agony. After some time, Latera emerged and noticed that the attackers were no longer anywhere to be found. This was terribly unnerving, but she assumed that the birds had probably scared them off for now. With the horses now gone, the crows too began to slowly but surely disperse from the scene. Shortly after, visibility was restored, and the sun once again shined brightly in the sky. It was hard for Latera to fathom how quickly the events had played out, but it was obvious that the road to the Tokali Hold—their version of the Great Fortress—would not be easily traveled any longer.

She turned and noticed Lennox walking through the grounds, expressionless and covered in dirt. Parish and Castor came to his side, but Castor seemed present only in body.

"How many are dead?" Lennox asked as she listened in.

Parish looked at him with befuddlement. "Chieftain, none of the men or women were killed," he said, seeming to not believe the words that came out of his own mouth.

Lennox remained expressionless and continued to not look in his councilman's direction as he spoke. "What about the fires?"

"It seems . . . " Parish struggled to get the words out. "It seems they were focused on tents filled with supplies. I suppose they mean to starve us," he whispered in despair.

The bad news just piled up too high for the disgraced Chieftain and he began to walk away.

While he did, he called out to those behind him, "Prepare everyone. We leave immediately."

Now with a small tear running down his cheek, Parish dreadfully replied, "Lennox, there is just one more thing." The Chieftain turned with a look that dared his councilman to give him worse news. "They have taken Walter Keagan."

CHAPTER 5

YOU CAN RUN

"What if he does not return, Malik?"

Malik turned to his wife, knowing that this sense of worry would not fully leave her until Elan had safely returned to the Hold.

"Whether he returns or not, Adila, what he wanted more than anything in the world was to do an act that would truly help his people," Malik reassured her as she paced through their home.

She was often a voice of reason, but recent events had her stressed, which in turn had Malik equally stressed. Her strength earned her great respect and provided the family political power among the Tokali clan members. It had been this way since he and Adila had come to the Hold just before Elan was born. They knew that out of all the smaller camps scattered across the open basin of the south, the largest of all the Tokali camps, located at the Murrieta's southernmost point, was the closest thing there was to a true city in the Territory besides the Great Fortress and held the best opportunities for their son.

And this journey had been his greatest opportunity yet.

"Someone needed to accept this responsibility, and you know as well as I do that there was no one more fit to do so than our Elan. Even if there had been, I doubt that boy would let them make the trip alone. He has dreamt of this kind of opportunity, this chance to be the champion of his people, his entire life, Adila."

"As much as I have dreaded it and feared for this day to come," she sighed. "I worry as any mother would. This is the most important time in the history of our people, and I just hope we made the right decision."

Malik contemplated her point the same way he had many times before. He knew his wife and he were getting older, as they approached middle-age, and he just hoped that their efforts would leave the next generation of Tokali in a safer, more peaceful position.

"It will certainly be something that will be debated among our people for all time, my love," he reflected. "Either way, I have nothing but pride in the bravery our boy has shown during this historical time for the Territory."

"So, too, will he be proud. I know this of course, and it comforts me that he succeeded in his quest thus far. He made it to the V'ahani and convinced them to travel to the Hold—that alone shows his strength," she replied, newly cheered. As they carried on with the same debate Malik was tired of having for days, a knock came to the door. "Who could that be at this hour?" Adila asked.

"That should be Pharaoh now. I told him I needed to speak with him," Malik replied. He felt exhausted at this point and was hungry, but this conversation was one that needed to be had. "Please, go put something together for the three of us. It will have been a long day for him as well."

"I will do so only if I will be able to know why this meeting is occurring," she agreed.

He grabbed her hands in his and promised, "Adila, when have you ever not been filled in on anything? Of course you will be a part of the conversation. Now please hear me when I beg you to relax about Elan. Our boy will make it back to us okay."

To this she nodded and slowly went away to follow his request. Though she was distressed lately and beginning to show signs of graying the same way he was, Malik found his wife to be as beautiful as the day he met her. There had always been a powerful aura about Adila, as well. It wasn't easily explained, but he best compared it to her eyes, whose shimmering gray-green colors did not seem to fade with time. Instead they evolved, as did she.

As Malik answered the door, he could hear her begin to prepare a meal for the two of them and their guest. He cracked the door open slowly to confirm it was Elan's friend Pharaoh. Once he did so, he promptly let him in.

"Pharaoh, how are you my boy?" he asked warmly once the door was shut behind the young man.

"I am as well as I can be while my friend is away," Pharaoh admitted. "As I mentioned to you earlier though, I have heard from the birds some news that I think you should hear."

"What news is that?" Adila suddenly chimed in. It appeared to Malik as if she was just waiting to pop out and show herself.

"Hello there, Mrs. Adila," Pharaoh greeted Adila with a hug.

"Some way to greet the boy," Malik scolded his wife. "Please forgive her, Pharaoh, she has been on edge as you can imagine."

"Not at all, sir," Pharaoh declared. "Now about the news that I heard . . ."

"Yes, what news did you hear?" Adila asked.

"Of course, we will surely hear about it shortly but please come sit down with us for a bit first," Malik said as he guided Pharaoh to their dining area.

Adila had now returned to cooking for them, of which he was glad because Malik had actually already heard the information. Earlier that day, Pharaoh confided in him that there was news that couldn't be shared directly, which Pharaoh would deliver that night. Malik became curious and asked around to his closest sources ahead of time what this might be. He soon discovered through rumor, which he was confident was correct, and was now trying to delay his wife's being informed as long as possible. He was stressed about how amplified her worry would become once she heard it for herself and wondered if there was some tiny sliver of hope that he could now get out of this without her finding out at all.

"Now please tell us first what is new with you," he said.

"Well, you know, much of the same lately," Pharaoh replied. "My parents are well, as are my brother and sister."

"Oh, that is very good to hear," Malik cheered. "And is your brother any closer to reaching his desired position as a guard?"

"Well, not since the last time we spoke," Pharaoh answered with his head slightly tilted.

"Yes, I suppose it does take some time to reach that point," Malik responded as soon as Pharaoh finished, speaking as slowly as he could. "I remember my days working my way up to earning the position. It was hard work, but eventually it paid off in the end, as I am most certain it has for you as well."

"Oh, it most definitely has," Pharaoh declared. "My parents and I could not be more proud."

"Yes I am sure they are quite proud," Malik said as the meat that Adila cooked began to simmer loudly. "Adila and I are proud as well."

"Thank you," Pharaoh replied awkwardly. "Uh, Malik, would you like me to let you know what I have heard from Elan now though?"

Just as Malik was about to jump at the opportunity to provide an affirmative with the volume of the prepared meal at its loudest, Adila whipped around. "Yes we would very much like to hear what you have heard now," she answered.

"Well hol—," Malik started.

"No," Adila interrupted him. "I know you know, Malik. Did you really think I would not see that? Pharaoh, tell me now. Is my boy all right? Is Elan alive?"

"Oh, yes, he is most definitely alive," Pharaoh answered. "Unfortunately though there has been an attack upon the group."

"By who? What happened?" Adila asked.

"By . . . by the Keagans. Walter Keagan, who was held by the V'ahani, was the reason for it. The Keagans had been after the group since the Riverlands to recover Walter, and they finally did through this swift assault. There were no casualties, but there was great loss of food and supplies. The V'ahani press on now needing to ration and possessing low morale. Their horses will be pushed to the brink to complete the remainder of the journey as quickly as possible. That was all the word he sent."

Malik's spirit sank as the details he'd heard were confirmed.

"Well this is . . . frustrating," Adila admitted. "I am sure you have an answer for how we should handle this, Malik?" she asked, angrily.

Malik honestly to that point had nothing despite his hours of knowledge of the situation. He didn't respond.

"Well I suppose not then," Adila said. "Anyway. We must take every action necessary to ensure that their journey south is successful. I believe that our best course is to call all Tokali to the Hold. All camps should be abandoned, including goods and supplies, so that the V'ahani may restock on whatever they come across. We have to be sure that they have what they need to make it here. Pharaoh, please send that word through the wind as silently as possible."

Malik felt ashamed for having not told his wife earlier. She had such a brilliant mind, and he knew he needed to offer some kind of apologetic solution. He stepped forward to finish for her and admit his shame.

"Please keep any spreading of news to an absolute minimum, Pharaoh. If you have anyone to share anything with, especially about our Elan, please bring it straight to us from here on out," he declared. "Along with the message she has requested, please also gather your friends to our home tomorrow evening. This news is dire, and it is my duty to prepare you boys for anything so we will be going on a special hunt."

With that, Pharaoh accepted their requests, and Adila passed him his meal. Malik watched as the young guard scarfed it down and subsequently rushed back home after thanking them. He knew that his wife's wrath would rain down upon him that night.

*

News of Walter's rescue pleased William. The eldest of the Keagan brothers was increasingly impressed by Clovis's effectiveness. Now that this problem was resolved, everything seemed to be going at least somewhat smoothly. With Daniel in place in the North, and the V'ahani of the Riverlands weakening, the Keagans could begin to expand their control without resistance. It would take time to forge the relationships, but with Daniel doing the talking and Clovis flexing their muscle, William knew they were in a great position.

After Walter had been retrieved, Clovis and his men had headed back to Fayette to regroup, and they were now in residence to discuss the next steps with William. They all shared in a large feast that evening to celebrate the men's return, and then, once the children were asleep, the adults regrouped in William's study. Mrs. Abigale went to bed, but the remainder of the party was eager to be in attendance. So, as William looked around the room, he met the eyes of Judith, Henry, Cassius, and Gregory, before continuing on to Clovis, Walter, and finally Devin Turpin, who had been invited to the feast due to his involvement in the entire chain of events.

William cleared his throat and began to address the group, who all had their evening drinks in hand.

"I'd just like to say, again, how grateful we are for y'all's safe return and to know Walter is clear of those brutes," he said as he turned to Clovis.

"Thank you, brother," Clovis replied. "But this is only the beginning, and we all understand that. Speaking of which," he added, turning to Cassius and the Abigales with a forced grin, "if you dear people wouldn't mind, we have some family business to discuss."

William cast a glance to Judith, who glared at him in response.

"That's okay, Clovis," he corrected, still looking at her, "Judith is a Keagan now, as are her kin. Whatever's to be discussed can be discussed with them present."

Judith sent William a grin of appreciation.

"Very well then," Clovis bemoaned. "Devin, if you could, please fill these Keagans in on what went down the past few days."

Devin recounted the tale of the recent timeline as it was originally told to William. With Clovis nodding along beside him, Devin retold the story that the Morrells fired the first shots on their men. Walter, who had now upgraded to a finely polished wooden walking cane, affirmed this point as well. Then Devin moved on to the details of the raid.

"Well, as for our daring rescue, along their travels the V'ahani took a pause in the night," he began. "We were mighty restless to get Walter here back to us so we pressed on. Eventually we caught up, but boy were we not expecting what came next! Perhaps it was more of a blessing than a curse though. Yes, I'd certainly like to think that it was a blessing! Anyhow, we prepared to ride in on horseback and create a scene chaotic enough to swipe Walter right on out of there. We had a good amount of help with that though, seeing as a whole hurricane of crows came and filled the sky like thunder clouds!" Devin said, looking at his audience for a reaction.

Unsurprisingly to William, no one reacted with any sort of shock or confusion.

"We saw the crows, as well," Judith followed.

"Saw them when?" Clovis asked.

"They passed over during the wedding reception," William

replied as he pondered the memory. "Quite a sight indeed but no more than a passing flock fortunately."

"Curious," Devin quipped. "They certainly did not pass over us. Nope, these crows came down with a fury as soon as we were upon the clansmen. The very air we breathed was filled with them, and in the frenzy nothing could be seen except the black of their feathers. It's a wonder we were able to snatch Walter up at all."

"But where does such a flock come from?" Gregory joined in.

"It was their own," Walter replied, answering what William thought to be a rhetorical question. "The crows brought messages from their relatives in the North. Before y'all came, I could hear them discussing it."

"You're saying that the birds carry their messages?" Henry blurted. "They surely got in your head when you were held captive!"

He looked around the room for someone to confirm that such notions were as ridiculous as they sounded but received no support.

"Forgive my father-in-law," William said. Turning to Henry he explained, "It's hard to understand at first for us Easterners. It certainly was for me. But these natives have a connection with this land. They can speak to its inhabitants in some cases and control them."

"Their most dangerous weapon is the bears," Clovis added. "In fact, one of them ripped apart the skull of one of our men."

"It is horrifying, I know," William said, again casting a glance at Judith. "But it's also a great opportunity if we can control the V'ahani."

"Which brings us to the next stage of our quest," Clovis said. "I know we've only just returned, but we left the V'ahani of the

Riverlands in a despairingly precarious state. I'd like very much to break their will, which would facilitate the opportunity for their capture. Walter also has a bit of intelligence, which might make winning their people over a bit easier once they're under our control, especially considering their vulnerable position."

William looked over at Walter.

"Yes, at the time of my being taken prisoner, it seems their leadership had a bit of an issue with the man in charge," he hummed. "Just when he was about to have me killed, those brutes staged a coup and shot their Chieftain into the river. I'd just finished telling him that his time had come, too!"

William nodded. "Nothing in this world makes me angrier than betrayal and deceit. Can't deny actually feeling for the Chieftain, but it is certainly another example that leadership is about enlisting people who will follow. Anyway, not to change the subject, but what of Jeannie Morrell? It was my understanding that the V'ahani held on to her when they captured Walter here. Were y'all not able to locate and snatch her up in the raid along with him?"

"They didn't capture her because she wasn't in the possession of the V'ahani," Walter answered. "I'm not sure who initiated it, but there was a very peculiar attack one night on their camp back up in the Riverlands. During said attack, Jeannie Morrell was taken."

"That is very peculiar," William said. "She could be anywhere at this point. Well, fuck it. Though it would be helpful to have her, I'm confident in Daniel's ability to make our connections nonetheless. Even if it does take longer, this has all been mostly good news and will factor in nicely once you're finished with the V'ahani. So continue on then, brother!" he cheered as he turned to Clovis.

"You've earned the right to make whatever spectacle you please of the situation. So I'll trust you with that. Just please remember that in the end we need them alive."

"As you wish, Billy," Clovis snickered.

"By the way, Walter, you sure you're up to continuing on with him?" William asked. "There'd be no shame in you staying and taking some time to recover from your injury until this deed's done."

Walter turned slowly to William.

"There isn't a wound on my body that could keep me from being there to help chase down those pitiful animals and see them shackled the same way they shackled me," he darkly exclaimed. "Whether they be physical chains, mental chains, or emotional, I will see to it that they are at the Keagan heel."

"I like your spirit, Walter," William chimed gleefully. "I'll see you soon then, my brothers!"

Clovis gestured to Devin and Walter, and the comrades left the room. Within the next few hours, they had assembled their men, and William watched them head off again to do what they did best. He was proud of what he and Daniel were able to do for Clovis in the Murrieta. It seemed to be working thus far both for his troubled younger brother and for the empire that he was building.

*

As they were with Pharaoh, Malik and Adila were close with many of their son's friends. From a young age, Elan's friend group had been tight-knit, and though each young man grew to have different responsibilities, their bond had remained strong. For that alone, Malik was proud of his son. He and Adila always tried to make sure the other boys felt welcome and were treated like their own sons whenever they were in their home. Malik knew, too, that many of them looked up to him, something Adila reminded him of often. So Malik made sure to see them regularly, and above all other things, always tried to be the elder who took them out for the Hold's weekly hunt. There was something about teaching the young men how to provide for the Hold that grew their confidence and their bond to one another.

Along with Pharaoh, a tall, intelligent young man who was a natural warrior, Elan's group consisted of Warrick, Hammond, and the brothers, Shelton and Gannon. Hammond and Shelton, like Pharaoh, were guards. This was a particularly common position for young Tokali men. However, Malik knew that the three all had different motivations for taking on the role.

While Pharaoh was a gallant warrior, Hammond was simply more of a thrill seeker, looking to do the most daunting task he could find. He always said that though he was very happy for Elan to have been chosen for his mission, he was also admittedly envious and longed for his own adventure.

Shelton, on the other hand, was much less interested in the act of being a guard and much more in the thought of it. A great motivation for him was the prestige of the position, which he felt would assist him in earning the favor of women despite his height, or lack thereof—a confidence he'd whispered to Malik one day after a particularly stinging rejection from a young Tokali woman.

Shelton's brother, Gannon, was also on the shorter side compared to their friends and unlike the guards whose hair was traditionally longer and kept in a bun, Gannon's was cut very short. He was much less concerned with prestige and much more concerned with using his hands. One of his favorite things to do was to put together and take apart weapons, and as he aged, Malik watched him become a very skilled craftsman. His skill in the creation of rifles carried over to his use of them, and he became widely known as one of the greatest marksmen in the Hold.

Lastly, there was Warrick. Warrick was a messy-haired artist but, in particular, his favorite thing to do was to write. People throughout the Hold enjoyed the stories he wrote using the tales others told as inspiration. When Elan first left for his trip, Warrick said that when the journey was complete, he would write his friend's story. It was going to be his greatest work, he promised, and all Tokali forever after would know the name Elan. Malik and Adila had appreciated the sentiment, and Malik noticed, not for the first time, that fame was something Warrick did not seem interested in for himself.

The night after Malik received the news from Pharaoh, the boys each arrived at Malik's home as requested. They all seemed excited for the hunt initially, but this would not be an ordinary hunt. Knowing the danger that Elan was in, which was seemingly going to follow him south, Malik knew the boys would need to grow up fast to represent the Tokali bravely. There would be no better test for the madness coming than the wild hogs. When the last of Elan's friends arrived, they gathered their hunting gear, and Malik led them to the outside of the Hold's northeast perimeter. As vital as each step in Elan's mission was, so, too, were the preparations Malik and Adila were trying to make at the Hold. As for the boys, whether they were ready to or not, he knew they would need to become men soon, a thought that was most prevalent on Malik's mind as they all traveled to meet the sun somewhere below the horizon.

A couple hours later, with the evening setting in and light beginning to dim, Malik and the boys had finally reached the hunting grounds. A thick, misty fog pervaded in the eerie wooded flatlands in which the hogs resided. Visibility at this time of day was low enough to be considered an advantage for the beasts.

In order to counter that, the group, Malik included, had all been taking turns calling to the wind to get their bearings as well as to practice the skill in general. Each had their struggles mastering that endeavor along the way, but Malik knew how important each part of that night's training would be. He needed to keep them grounded and focused on the task at hand, especially Hammond, who was the least patient of the bunch.

As Hammond continuously failed to receive any response in trying to locate the first boar, he whined, "Someone else should try this first, just so we can do some kind of hunting tonight!"

"It must be you, Hammond," Malik challenged him. "When things do not go your way you must not quit or you will learn nothing. The only way to truly fail is to surrender."

"Yeah, but there is no time. Elan will be here with the V'ahani before we know it and what if I am too far behind?" he replied.

"You are no further behind than any of us," Malik assured him. "The only thing that makes a task impossible to accomplish for a person is their own mind telling them it is impossible. Just remember that when yours does try to suggest that to you, that you must above all else keep yourself at ease."

Hammond nodded and took a deep breath. As he looked up to the sky he breathed again and muttered the word "ease" to himself. Malik looked down at him happily as the young man went to a knee. Hammond again called up to the wind. They waited a few seconds until finally a response came.

Hammond smiled ear-to-ear when he heard a sparrow reply to tell them to continue a bit further east. The other boys all congratulated him enthusiastically. Malik always tried to instill the wisdom in them that they each had different skills, some of which came easier than others, so that no judgment would pass among them. Moments like that made him feel successful to that end.

They continued east as the sparrow advised and surely enough, soon came upon their first hog. The boys muttered among each other when they spotted it—it was much larger than they anticipated. Though it was simply grazing, it still appeared ferocious. It breathed heavily, snorting occasionally, and more than anything else, its tusks were its most intimidating attribute.

Malik guided the group to cover as he began instructing them in the faintest whisper.

"You will not learn to harness the fear of imminent death from afar, only when it comes straight for you," he proclaimed. "In order to prepare you for that, you will each be taking a hog one-on-one. Gannon, you will go first. You will pop out from cover with your rifle and fire at the beast upon approach. But be prepared, these animals are ferocious warriors. Expect them to be ruthless, and, if you miss, it will show you no mercy. In the case that you do miss, be prepared with your dagger. If that fails, we will try our best to help you, but until that time this is your burden to bear. Lastly, I want you to all know that fear is exactly what you should be feeling right now. However, you must remember what I said to Hammond. Your greatest adversary is your own self-doubt. Overcome that, and the pig will fall."

Malik looked at all of the boys after this announcement. He expected them to be shaking in fear, but was surprised to find them all still. Gannon breathed deeply with his eyes closed, clenching his gun. He looked down at it, then up at the other boys, and then to Malik. He took one last breath and left their cover. The others drew their rifles as Gannon walked out to face the hog. As it heard him, it began a most horrid squealing, as if it was already being tortured just by Gannon's presence. The monster rapidly charged in his direction just as he lifted his rifle toward it. He aimed down his sight straight at the large mass barreling toward him—but did not shoot. It drew closer and closer and was soon within 100 feet of him. An instant later, it was at fifty feet, but Malik watched as the boy still stood unmoving. The other boys began flinching, tense and fidgeting, though they remained undercover with their weapons raised as the boar barreled towards Gannon. Suddenly, a crack rang out from Gannon's rifle. Malik could see a bullet hole drilled straight through the animal's skull. Somehow its momentum was so great that it still continued forward, sliding dead to the young man's feet. Gannon had succeeded.

If they weren't still on a hunt, Malik would have erupted with praise, but he contained himself and joined the others in giving Gannon an enthusiastic, but silent, pat on the back. Before they got too comfortable, Malik was sure to inform them that Pharaoh and

Shelton were next. When their targets were found, the next two boys did not have kills that were quite as clean as Gannon's, but they got the job done. Pharaoh first slowed his beast down significantly with two shots that created near fatal wounds. As his prize came stumbling toward him he was able to wrestle its weakened body to the ground, at which point he removed his blade and slit its throat.

Shelton, on the other hand, seemed to have had a stroke of luck. When he emerged from cover, his pig didn't even notice. He was able to get his first shot off on an unmoving target but still missed badly, which he unfortunately repeated on his second try. As the creature drew nearer, however, he fired one last bullet, which landed directly in the hog's eye. Afterwards, he admitted to Malik that at the time he'd been unsure as to whether the final bullet had even connected.

The last two remaining were Warrick and Hammond. Warrick confessed his nerves to Malik as the group moved on to find the next hog, and Malik strived to reassure him.

"Before my son left on his journey, he would rave about how glad he was that his story would be in writing thanks to you, Warrick," he said with his hand on the boy's shoulder. "What you are living right now though, this is not the tale of Elan. It does not belong to anyone other than you, and surely, as a writer, you must know that each of us has a story that deserves to be told. Now is your chance to start your own."

Warrick looked out from their cover at his challenger. Finally, he worked up the courage and emerged. Like Shelton's, his first shot missed badly. His arms were shaking as the rage of his hog filled the air. Its cries rang through the night. He aimed his rifle and fired again. This shot did graze his target, but only partially slowed it down. It also increased the intensity of the screeching. Warrick now stood frozen. He soon began to stumble as he lowered his hand to his dagger. The hog thwarted his feverish attempt to turn and run, tackling him to the ground. Malik started to prepare himself to intervene, worried that Warrick would not be able to fight back. The animal on top of the boy was thrashing furiously, but as Malik rose from cover to launch himself into the fray, he saw that Warrick was in fact holding the beast back with one hand and reaching for his blade with the other. Once the blade was in his grasp, he dug it into the side of the pig, which began roaring in pain. Just before Malik could rejoice, he realized that the blow was still not fatal. With a quick sway of its head, the hog's tusk swiped at Warrick's shoulder. The boy screamed at a pitch that competed with his enemy's.

Malik had finally seen enough. He looked to Gannon, and the craftsman took action. His bullet zoomed right past Warrick and silenced the hog. The injured boy was writhing in pain. Malik rushed to his side.

"It is okay, Warrick. You are going to be all right," he encouraged him. "Go get something from our bags to wrap his arm!" he called to the others. "You did great, Warrick. This was the first time you faced your fears, and you did it head on. Your story has begun, my friend."

"I—ah—I suppose it has," he replied with a smile through the pain.

After Warrick was all patched up and calmed down, Malik turned to Hammond, "Are you ready?"

"Are we still going to continue after what happened?" Pharaoh questioned. "I am not prepared to see my friends hurt again."

"Of course we are," Malik answered. "Let me tell you all something, and if you disagree, then we can go back right now," he said as he faced them. "I can see in each of you tonight a new light—a light that exists because you looked death right in the face, and you walked away standing taller than before. You all acquired a new knowledge on this hunt, not just of combat, but of who you are on the inside. Whether it be Warrick realizing that he has his own story to tell, Gannon finding his connection to his weaponry, Pharaoh learning to finish what he's started, or Shelton discovering that luck is a finite resource. You all found something. Now, as I said, if any of you would disagree with that, then we can be on our way. But if you do not, how could you take this opportunity of self-discovery that you were just given away from your friend?"

Pharaoh turned to Hammond. "He is right," he declared. "It is your turn, Hammond."

Hammond picked up his rifle. Once the final hog had been found, Hammond looked at the group one last time for assurance and confidently emerged from the final set of bushes. Like Shelton, he did not alert this final massive hog when he crept out. With his head held high, he lifted his rifle, breathed deeply, and with the sight pointed directly for the kill shot, he pulled the trigger. What came next was only a rifle-jamming click, but it was one that was just loud enough for the beast to hear. Hammond took a step back and flinched as the now raging hog rushed toward him full force. Malik could see the, "why me," written all over him. Yet as the pig barreled closer, Hammond once again stood tall.

"Ease," Malik could see him whisper as he steadied himself. His stance shifted to prepare for his charging foe with his knife now at the ready. "Ease," he repeated again, this time louder. As the pig charged, it progressively increased the volume of its horrid whining. Hammond followed suit as he continued to repeat the word. "Ease. Ease. Ease! Ease!" He yelled louder and louder until finally his tone was even higher than that of the pig. "EASE!" He screamed one last time as he stared it dead in the eye. The hog abruptly began to slow down and quiet as it closed the gap between them. Hammond, along with the rest of the group in cover, was frozen at the hog's reaction. Finally, the pig came to a full, peaceful stop in front of him and stood still.

Malik emerged slowly from their hiding place and came toward him. He was in utter shock as he moved toward Hammond's hog, which did not make a single sound in response. He couldn't comprehend it. The V'ahani carried stories of controlling animals in their lore, but the Tokali never had—had never gone beyond calling the wind. In fact, Malik did not even believe the stories to be true . . . at least he hadn't until this moment. For a few minutes, Malik circled the hog and then looked toward a still motionless Hammond.

With a stutter he asked, "My boy . . . How—how did you . . . ?"

Hammond looked toward his second father with a radiating grin. "I do not know," he responded.

Gasping in disbelief, Malik turned to the others. "This is too powerful of a gift for anyone to know about right now before we come to understand it ourselves," he declared. "Word of what happened here does not leave this group. Is that clear?"

The boys nodded blankly, the attention of all fixed on the hog, which remained perfectly still.

*

Jeannie lay awake as night was just beginning to shift into morning. She couldn't sleep and noticed Hanzah across the room was restlessly shifting his weight. He turned over toward her.

"Are you having trouble sleeping too?" he asked her.

"Yeah," she confirmed.

"Are you scared?" Hanzah whispered.

"I don't think so," Jeannie replied. "My entire family, everything I ever knew, was burned to the ground before my eyes, so I'm not entirely sure I have anything left to be afraid of."

"Well, to be honest with you, I am afraid, Jeannie," he said. She felt respect bloom for his sincerity and shifted, getting herself comfortable to listen in. "In our culture, sons follow in the footsteps of our fathers quite literally. We learn from their every move because we are there to witness their every move. That morning, when the councilmen first fired their weapons, I felt something strange. I found myself not wanting to jump into that river. It was entirely against my upbringing that I did so. What I actually wanted, I think, and what I should have done was to remain right there and be shot dead alongside my father. I had been with him my entire life, and he was more-so my home than the Riverlands itself."

Jeannie hadn't believed until now that there was anyone who could understand her sorrow. She tried to comfort him by saying the same things she would want to be told. "That isn't strange at all," she implored. "In fact, I felt the same thing when my mother sent me off into the woods. I only did it because I could tell that my safety would be the last thing she would ever feel good about. She knew the end was coming, and I couldn't deny her that last bit of joy. As I ran and looked back, though, there was no other place I would have rather been than by my family's side in their final moments. As for your instinct to escape, it wasn't an accident either. That's what your father taught you. It's what he would've wanted you to do. But I can promise you one thing that I've learned and am sure of, Hanzah," she continued as she saw him move to sit up in his cot. "There is a reason why we didn't die there with them. We escaped in order to restore the mountains that they raised, to grow them even higher than they were before, and to cut down those who wished to take what wasn't theirs at our expense."

"Mountains they raised?" Hanzah asked.

"Um, yeah . . . I mean like . . . just the things they achieved," Jeannie answered, confused about what he wasn't following.

"Oh, okay. Yes, of course, you are right," he uttered. "There is nothing I have thought about more than my people and ensuring that the last thing the councilmen and Keagans ever see is the eyes of the grizzlies as they are torn apart."

Jeannie basked in the thought.

"Then it's settled," she declared. "And we must hold each other to those ends."

Just as Hanzah was about to reply, the door to the bedroom burst open. Dominic came in, rushing frantically towards them.

"Children, we must gather our things and leave now," he whispered loudly. "There's no time to waste!"

After what had unfolded outside the saloon, Jeannie felt a hint of uncertainty about Dominic's guidance. The position she was put in there had been a dangerous one and one she did not want to be pushed into again. However, she was also hit with curiosity as they hurriedly followed his lead and organized their belongings.

"Is something wrong again?" she asked.

"Not necessarily, yet, but there have been some developments, and with Daniel Keagan in town . . . we simply must be leaving. I can explain later," he answered in a frantic, rushed tone.

Jeannie only had so many belongings to carry and was soon waiting patiently by the door beside Hanzah. A few minutes later, after gathering some things of his own, Dominic met them there.

"So, how will we ensure that we escape unseen?" Hanzah asked.

Jeannie was still stuck on the saloon incident and wondered the same thing.

"We won't be escaping yet," Dominic said as he made last minute adjustments to his shoes and coat. "We have a very brief stop we need to make first."

Jeannie was now utterly confused and cast a look towards Hanzah to see he wore the same expression as her own. "If this involves knives being hurled at me in the dark again, then I can't follow you, Dominic," she declared. "You have to tell me where we're going! What could be more important than escaping?"

"I agree with Jeannie," Hanzah declared. "You have been quite helpful so far, at least for the most part, but that was unreasonable to ask of her last night."

"Look, I'm terribly sorry for that, Jeannie, but I truthfully didn't know what else to do at the time," Dominic said. "I know you're confused and probably scared, but right now you have to trust me, all right? This detour is one we must take. I beg you to trust me on this, and I promise everything will make sense very soon."

Jeannie steadily nodded, and again they turned together to follow Dominic's lead. The night was silent with the exception of crickets screeching and the wind blowing as Dominic covertly maneuvered them through the streets to a familiar house. A small part of her relaxed then—at least this place would be friendly. Dominic snuck them up to the door, scanning the area first. Then he knocked in an odd pattern, and the door swung open. In the doorway stood two women, which Jeannie immediately recognized as Debra and Cassie Kennedale. The eccentric sisters rushed all three of them inside, and then surrounded Jeannie in a huge hug. Tears began to roll down their faces, a reaction which she did not fully understand, though she was very pleased to see more people she knew. She wrapped her arms around them in response, and though she didn't know the ladies incredibly well, the embrace warmed her soul.

When they backed away and looked at her, their smiles appeared big enough to break their freckled faces.

"I'm sorry, little lady," Cassie said wiping her eyes. "I know you must be startled, but we knew your parents very well, and we're just so happy that you're alive and doing all right."

"Yes, I can certainly second that," Debra added. "It's always so good to see a Morrell face."

"Thank you," Jeannie said with her hand on her heart. "Your words and warmth mean so much to me."

Jeannie noticed a look pass between Dominic and the

Kennedales before the sisters jumped into motion.

"Please," Debra addressed the group as she had already begun to walk away, "follow us."

Jeannie looked to Dominic, who ushered her forward, as she turned and followed Debra and Cassie through a hallway and up a flight of stairs with Hanzah and Dominic behind her. At the top of the stairs, there was a colorful but oddly decorated room.

"What is this strange place?" Hanzah asked.

"This is where we do our fortune telling," Debra replied. "We call it the 'Tomorrow Room' to our clients. It looks this way to add to the mystique of the experience. Please, pay it no mind. We didn't bring you here to tell you your fortune, but rather, to show it to you."

The sisters pulled away a section of curtain that covered one of the walls to reveal a door.

They looked at the children with a twinkle in their eyes, and Cassie whispered, "Before this door is opened, you must promise to remain quiet. Remember, this town is not safe right now, and if we are found now, then it could mean the end of us all."

Jeannie nodded. Once she received their confirmation, Cassie turned and knocked on the door in the same pattern Dominic used when they arrived. Soon after, it opened from the inside and a figure slowly emerged. Jeannie felt the bag she'd been clutching drop to the floor. Standing before her alive and well was her eldest brother, Harrison Morrell.

CHAPTER 6

GOSSAMER

"Jeannie . . . you're alive," Harrison choked.

As soon as the air had returned to her lungs, Jeannie launched herself at her brother, embracing him as if she'd never let go again.

"I saw it burn, Harrison," she cried. "I saw it burn to the ground and they were all inside." She knew that her words must be nearly incoherent behind her long sobs. But she looked up at him again, feeling as if she was seeing a ghost. "You were inside," she whispered, now shivering as she ducked her head back into his chest. "Mother told me she was going to go upstairs to get you and Donovan."

"I'll explain, sister," he said in a tone that suggested he himself was equally emotional. He put his hand on her chin to lift her face toward his and told her, "But right now I'm just so glad you're all right, and I want you to know I'm here now. You're not alone anymore."

His words filled her with warmth. "You can't leave me again, Harrison," she demanded. "You have to promise."

Chuckling he assured her, "Just as intense as ever. I promise, Jeannie. I'm not going anywhere."

After a few minutes where Jeannie just clung to Harrison, she recalled all the people in the room and disentangled herself.

Harrison nodded to her and the others and motioned for them all to take a seat at the round table in the Tomorrow Room. Jeannie noticed a shade of light stubble across her older brother's face then, and that his short, typically combed-over hair was a bit of a mess. He was usually very neat, but his dress shirt was untucked, his pants seemed a bit looser, and his clothes were dirty. It might've hurt Jeannie to see him so disheveled, but all that mattered to her at the moment was that he was alive.

"They saved me," Harrison started as he turned to the Kennedales. The sisters nearly jumped out of their seats at the mention. "That morning was the first of the week, so it was a delivery morning, Jeannie. That's why I wasn't upstairs. Mother must've thought I had come back by that time because that day I had an early start. I never did make it home though, thanks to Cassie and Debra."

He sent them a grateful smile, and Jeannie felt her appreciation of the sisters grow even more.

"I was making my last stop at the home of Charles Langston," he continued. "That man was rambling more than I've ever heard him ramble before. He was going on and on about the Keagans and how father should just let them have what they wanted. 'They're not the kind to be given a difficult time' he kept telling me. It was odd, I'd heard quite a bit about them that morning from several people in Harran, but I never did see them. I suppose I figured it was just the townsfolk telling stories as they always did. Clearly, I was wrong. Soon after, while I was still in Charles's home, we saw the smoke rising. I ran out toward it as fast as I could. I nearly made it, too, but the Kennedales intercepted me."

Cassie turned with a scowl to Dominic. "That's why that chicken shit Charles Langston has it out for us," she growled. "When we saw Harrison running toward the smoke, we went straight after him, because we knew what happened as soon as we saw it. Charles was standing out on his porch like a puppy pretending to be a watchdog. He yaps like one, too, that little bitch."

"Then he knows you were hiding Harrison?" Jeannie asked, a chill rushing down her spine.

"Oh no, dear girl," Debra assured her. "We weren't the only ones in Harran running to see why smoke was rising from the Morrell home, you can be sure of that. He just wants to feel important and knowledgeable."

Jeannie slowly released her breath, letting her shoulders relax again.

"I didn't want to let them take me, but the sisters wouldn't let me go back to the house under any circumstances," Harrison said, returning to his story. "If it wasn't for the horror I was feeling, I would've been much more appreciative at the time. But in that moment, the smoke was clouding my judgment."

"Don't you worry about that," Debra said. "We couldn't even imagine how hard it must've been, and so we expected your resistance."

Dominic turned to the sisters and said, "Well, you're both heroes, and I'm sure I speak for everyone when I say we're all grateful. However, there's now the matter of our next move—and we must discuss it immediately. We need to decide quickly and be on our way. If we don't leave this town, it'll only be a matter of time before we're found, which isn't an option after what occurred last night."

"What happened last night?" Debra asked.

Jeannie's eyes jumped to Dominic.

"We ran into some trouble on the way which . . . well, unfortunately it ended in my killing a Keagan man," he explained as he looked down and cracked his knuckles.

"You did what you needed to do for Hanzah and me," Jeannie said, before Dominic could think much of the group's silence. Since he delivered on his promise of a safe stop, she felt grateful to him and an urge to defend him. "It couldn't have been an easy choice, but the Keagan man was threatening us, so Dominic had no other option."

"Thank you, Jeannie," Dominic replied. "He's buried out in the woods, about fifty paces in if you enter directly between my house and Charles's. He's underneath a stake that I left. It's only a matter of time before they start to worry, so we must move quickly."

"I do not mean to be selfish, but I must go north to the Mountainlands, whether you all come with me or not. I must warn my people," Hanzah suddenly blurted, having been silent since Harrison emerged from the wall.

Jeannie wanted to go with him. She meant the pact they had made, but she wasn't on her own anymore, either. She glanced at Harrison, who was looking at Hanzah curiously.

"I'm sorry," Harrison said, "I don't think I've asked, and not to be rude, but we haven't met yet. Who are you?"

"This is Hanzah," Dominic answered before Hanzah could. "He's a V'ahani and the son of the Chieftain of the Riverlands who, most unfortunately, was also murdered on the morning the Keagans descended upon your family's home. I came across Hanzah by the River White, and he was instrumental in rescuing your sister from the V'ahani traitors who had captured her."

"Oh my goodness, I remember you from our fathers' dealings together! You're the son of Chieftain Arkouda!" Harrison declared.

"Yes, I am," Hanzah replied somberly.

Harrison stood and walked up to him before reaching out his hand.

"I'm very sorry for your loss, Hanzah," he offered as they shook. "Our fathers were great allies and had nothing but respect for one another. Hopefully we can restore the alliance our families shared once I reclaim the Morrell name in these parts! Until then though I can't thank you enough for saving my sister." He then turned to Dominic as well and added, "I can't thank either of you enough, and I'm forever in your debt. I will repay you, Hanzah. I'll help you reach your people in the Mountainlands. It will be a great way for me to establish a relationship with the rest of your leaders, as well. But then again, before we make this dangerous trek, I must ask, how can you be sure we'll be safe if we do successfully arrive, given what's happened to your father?"

Hanzah took a deep breath and answered, "My uncle Orrin is a Chieftain in the Mountainlands. The councilmen who betrayed my father have surely sent lies north. However, if my uncle and his people were to see me alive and hear my words directly, then they will know the truth. The people of the Riverlands are traveling south now with the intent of uniting with the Tokali. Despite what they have done, I hope they do merge with them as soon as possible. My sister, Latera, is with them, and I need to reach my people in the North so I can work with them to ensure she is brought home safely from the Hold.

"As you mentioned, there is also personal incentive for you to come with me," he continued, splitting his glance between Harrison, Dominic, and Jeannie. "The unification was requested with the purpose of going on the offensive against the Keagans. My people wanted to join the Tokali so that we could have a large presence with which to attack them from two fronts. Somewhat of a strangling-type strategy on their central location in Fayette. You can help us see that through, and I promise you my people will know that you did when it's over. The Morrells will be restored in the North, and Dominic, Debra, and Cassie you will also be most graciously thanked however you would see fit."

Hanzah paused a moment to let that sink in.

"I do hope you come," he continued. "It will be a perilous journey for me to make on my own, even though I know the way, and I would appreciate the company. But I understand whatever you decide."

The others looked around the room at one another.

"Strangling the Keagans sounds nice," Dominic joked.

"Agreed," Jeannie chirped in reply, new hope blooming inside her. "All in favor?" she asked. Gentle cheers rang out from all but the Kennedales. Jeannie turned to them, her mood dampening a notch. "Are you not coming with us?"

"I'm afraid we won't be of any assistance on the journey north, love," Cassie said. "Our place is here where we can keep tabs on Harran for when you return. This way when you do, we'll know all about those you can trust and those you can't."

"But what if they give you trouble?" Dominic asked. "The bastards already have."

The same question was on Jeannie's mind. If the Keagans could take the lives of her family, would they have any qualms about hurting more people?

"We greatly appreciate what you did for us Dominic," Debra replied. "But we'll be okay here for now. My sister and I are a pair of wolves. As long as we're together, we're strong—and we'll make sure you always have a place in Harran if you need it. Just make sure when you come back, it's to drive these demons out."

"Yes, please," Cassie cheered. "We'd like our home back."

"Very well then. Best of luck to you both and we'll see you soon," Dominic said.

Jeannie could not have been more appreciative of the Kennedales. After she gave each of the sisters a hug, she told them so.

"Thank you for all you've both done—and thank you for returning my brother to me."

The sisters smiled first at her and then at Harrison.

"Of course, my dear child," Debra replied.

Jeannie turned to Hanzah then. "We're with you, Hanzah."

Hanzah nodded in acknowledgment.

"Yes, indeed," Dominic added. "My friends, we're off to the Mountainlands."

With that, they prepared their things and approached the door to depart.

"They'll surely be patrolling to keep track of what comes in and out of Harran," Harrison said. "How will we slip past them?"

"Don't worry about that," Dominic whispered coyly, though Jeannie nearly sighed, as she was eager to know the answer to that question, as well.

Dominic seemed awfully secretive about his plans, and she was starting to wonder if the others would keep being left in the dark.

"I'll take care of everything," he said. "Just stay close to me and take these." He reached into a sack and pulled out three pistols with holsters to match. His own set was already around his own waist. "I assume you all know how to use these?" He asked as they nodded and strapped them on. "Good—just in case," he said with a wink. "Now we'll go to my house first to retrieve Nala and her trailer to hide you in. Once we do, you'll simply need stay covered until we're far enough out of town."

His air of confidence still didn't keep Jeannie from being worried. However, before she knew it, he opened the door, and they were off. The group snuck over to his home without drawing any attention. They then came upon his barn. Nala muttered as he saddled her up, putting Jeannie on edge with every sound that the steed emitted.

Soon enough, Nala was tied up, and her trailer attached. Dominic guided them in underneath a sheet with the rest of their belongings. Now they would just have to lie and wait. The tension built as Jeannie worried about whom might be on the other side of the sheet the next time it was lifted. She shifted around to try to get comfortable, tucked her short hair behind her ear, and then, they were moving. The trailer treaded along slowly as it rolled away from Dominic's home and through the main road. The town felt empty, and evidence of the sun's existence had only just begun to appear through the sheet. After some time of hearing nothing but the rolling of the cart and trotting of the horse, Jeannie started to feel better about the plan. She thought that they must be close to exiting Harran by now. Then she heard a voice. She felt some relief to know it was Dominic's as she peeked through the tiniest opening in the sheet.

"Evening, sir," he called out.

His greeting was met by the response of a sleepy man standing guard who attempted to wake himself while the horse approached. "Where might you be headed at this hour?" The man yawned.

Jeannie spotted the lion's paw pin on the man's chest as Dominic replied, "I'm heading west. The nature of my craft will take me out there for a performance that I must make by mid-day, so that's why I'm headed out so early."

The story would check out as they purposely traveled out of Harran in the western side of town to hide their northern travel intentions.

The man squinted at Dominic. "Wait a second," he said. "Are you the magician from the saloon earlier?"

"Precisely!" Dominic cheered.

"Well shoot, I saw you there. You might not remember me, but we met briefly. My name is Collin McCormack, to reintroduce myself. Anyways, have a good performance," he replied with a smile as he stepped back.

Jeannie was baffled at the ease of the exchange outside the cart.

"No, I do vaguely remember you Collin, but nice to meet you again! Thank you for the well-wishing, and I'll be seeing you soon," Dominic replied before he snapped the reins, ushering Nala forward.

The cart shifted forward, and Jeannie sighed quietly in relief.

"Wait!" Collin reprimanded. "Wait! Not yet!"

The cart came to an abrupt stop as Dominic replied, "Oh sorry, Collin, was there something else?"

"It's all right. It's my fault there for wishing you luck before I was ready to let you go!" Collin cleared his throat. "But I'll be needing to check your trailer before you leave, or my people will have my head, you know. But as soon as I do, then yes, you may be on your way again."

Jeannie nearly gasped but held it in. She heard the steps as Collin came trotting over to the wagon. At first he could be heard proceeding to Nala where Jeannie spotted him petting the horse smoothly. Then he slowly crept toward the back. Jeannie cringed as she heard him dragging his hand along the wooden side of the wagon. The sound was slow and rough against his gloves.

Dominic swiftly replied, "That should be fine, sir! But for your kindness, how about a trick first?"

"Oh yes, please," Collin said as he yawned again. "There really isn't much to see out here, so some entertainment would be great!"

"Great then!" Dominic called, climbing down from the wagon.

He then reached into the carriage for something right by Jeannie's head. She ducked down but followed him with her eyes. His hand emerged with a flask and something else that he kept hidden. Jeannie didn't move but watched out of the small slit in the sheet's material.

Approaching Collin, Dominic asked, "Have you ever heard of dragons and their ability to breathe fire?"

"Yes, of course!" the man chirped.

"Good," Dominic said warmly, now within arms-length of the man. "You see, dragons are mostly believed to be a myth. However, there's evidence in some people on this earth that dragons live on."

The guard responded with sarcastic disbelief. Then Dominic paused and froze before cracking his knuckles again.

"So how about it?" the man impatiently asked, breaking Dominic's trance.

Dominic jumped a little. "Right," he replied. "First let me take a drink. It is a heavy task to summon the dragon within me and I like to be as relaxed as I can be." He took a swig, then reached his hand to his mouth and blew a stream of fire just over Collin's head.

The guard ducked quickly and then looked up in awe at the flame flowing over him. "Oh my goodness!" he yelled.

Jeannie began to sweat as she noted what a commotion Dominic was causing. As soon as the blinding fire disappeared from Collin's eyes, however, Dominic jumped in front of him and forcefully delivered two fingers directly between his eyebrows. The already sleepy man immediately passed out and came crashing to the ground. Jeannie watched in shock as Dominic got right back up on the carriage and, in quite a hurry, urged Nala along, truly beginning the journey north.

*

Charles Langston sat fidgeting anxiously in the lobby of the hotel as he awaited the arrival of Daniel Keagan. The man who greeted Daniel briefed him on the story Charles had told. As soon as the sun rose into the sky that morning, Charles had apparently gotten himself ready in the finest clothes he had. He then scurried on over for what he described to the man as a "discussion of the utmost importance and urgency."

Daniel peered through a window to see Charles' leg tapping without pause as he furiously kept fixing the hair on the sides of his balding head. From his chair he looked high and low around the room. It was as if he thought there was a chance Daniel might be hiding somewhere, like if Charles professed what he knew an instant sooner, it could keep the entire place from exploding. The Keagan brother rolled his eyes at the thought. He was in no rush to meet this man.

Only a half hour or so after Charles had abruptly arrived, Daniel finally entered the room.

"Daniel!" Charles shouted, sounding half exasperated.

"Hello there, Charles," Daniel said with a crooked grin. "Forgive me, I know we spoke once previously, but remind me of your occupation here in Harran please?"

"Oh, uh, yes sir," Charles replied, furrowing his brows. "You might remember that I'm the mayor here."

The memory suddenly snapped back to Daniel. "Oh yes, of course!" he replied. "What can I do for you Mr. Mayor?" His veiled mocking went right over Charles' head, and he knew it, so he figured he'd keep it going as long as he could. Entertainment came in strange forms in this town.

"Well, sir," Charles began, "I want you to understand that I take your acceptance of my role very seriously, and I'll uphold it with the greatest responsibility. That being said," he continued, "as you know with me being in a high position here in this town for as long as I have been, I'm well aware of the intentions of its inhabitants. I hear things is what I'm trying to say, and quite frankly, I have reason to believe that there are some people here who mean to not accept the Keagans."

Finally, Daniel was interested, and his concentration focused more firmly on the man, though he still wasn't taking him entirely seriously. "Is that right?" he asked. "Please continue."

"Yes of course," Charles chirped. "Well I'm not sure if you've met the Kennedale sisters yet, but they've been acting mighty peculiar since the Keagans arrived in town. I might even go as far as to say they're unhappy that you've come! I mean . . . you clearly came here to help us, so I don't understand it! But when I spoke to them they had nothing nice to say and made ludicrous accusations."

"What kind of accusations?" Daniel asked. At the very least the gossip was beginning to amuse him.

"Well, sir, for one thing, they suggested that the Morrell home was burned down intentionally!" he exclaimed, which made Daniel genuinely curious. "They're clearly delusional, aren't they?"

A response didn't come immediately as Daniel considered what this oafish man had just said to him. He knew his brother Clovis, and he began to think of how possible it might be that the youngest Keagan burned the Morrell house to the ground without provocation. Then he realized who he was talking to and decided not to jump to conclusions about his own blood.

"Of course, that's a ridiculous suggestion. We had no desire to kill the Morrells. But why do you think they'd make such a claim?" he asked.

"Of that I'm not entirely sure, Mr. Daniel," he said sulking. "But I believe they're hiding something."

"Hiding what?" Daniel asked swiftly, looking away.

Charles looked down at the floor. "I'm not sure, sir. Again, I just don't trust them, and I believe their attitude will bring about the destruction of this town."

Daniel had heard what he needed to hear. "I understand, and I thank you Charles Langston," he said with exaggerated seriousness. "I haven't quite had the opportunity to speak to everyone in Harran yet, but I'll certainly talk to the Kennedales today and see if what you say about them is true."

"It is true," Charles blurted.

This man irritated Daniel more than his typically patient self was accustomed to. ". . . Okay, Charles. I believe you. Thanks again for this information, Mr. Mayor," Daniel replied, trying desperately to transition to the farewell. Never before did he have so much trouble feigning respect for a person, yet the man was still in awe of him.

"You're most welcome, sir," Charles squeaked. "Any time I can be of service to the Keagans, please just let me know."

The two stood up, and Daniel half-heartedly shook his hand. "We should be able to handle things here, but thanks again. If we need you, we'll come to you."

With that, they parted ways. Daniel had a lot to think about as he retired to his room, which was surprising considering the source of his information. As much as he didn't want to accept it, he realized that this would not be the last time he heard from Charles Langston.

*

The rest of Daniel's day remained as busy as his days always were. Later on, though, he found some open time to investigate Charles' rambling suspicions about the Kennedale sisters and marched toward their home. As much as Charles had put him off on a personal level, Daniel actually was rather excited to explore the depths of foolish drama that shrouded this not-so-simple town. Even if the fears of these women did go unfounded, he was always learning about people.

There was not an immediate answer to his first knock on the Kennedale door, and he began to worry that the sisters weren't home. However, just before he gave it another try, the door cracked to show a woman carefully peering through.

"Hello there! I don't mean to be a bother to y'all, but my name is Daniel Keagan," he said in a cheerful voice. As the first sister opened the door a bit wider, the second was looking on from behind. Daniel peered in to inspect the inside of the house as much as he could. "I'm sure y'all have heard by now, but my family will be playing a major role in overseeing safe commerce here in Harran, as well as all of the Riverlands, and I'm here to ensure everything goes as smoothly as possible. I was wondering if I might come in and have a word to discuss this further with you ladies."

"Yeah," the sister at the door whispered. "Come in."

Daniel giddily walked through the door as if he were entering the home of an old friend. "Much appreciated!" He cheered as they led him to their table.

"Something to drink?" Cassie asked. Both sisters spoke in short bursts of sentences.

"Yes, please, certainly!" he replied. "Now, it's my understanding that you two would be the sisters, Ms. Debra and Cassie Kennedale.

If that is the case, might I ask which of you would be Cassie and which is Debra?"

"I'm Cassie," the sister who hadn't answered the door indicated as she delivered three cups of water to the table.

Daniel immediately marched over to her. "Very nice to meet you Cassie," he greeted, grabbing her hand tightly with both of his and giving her a kiss on the cheek. He then turned to Debra. ". . . And that must make you Debra!" he said, turning to her with his arms reached out toward her and repeating his gesture. Daniel's jolly demeanor was entirely intentional despite the sisters' lack thereof. He could tell quickly that whether Charles was right or wrong, these Kennedales were guarded.

When Debra tried to step out of his embrace, he let her do so, but kept a tight hold of her wrist. Looking closely at it, he noticed it was bandaged. "What happened here?" he asked with an exaggerated gasp.

Daniel deduced from their modest looks and harsh personalities that affectionate attention likely wasn't something these two were used to. Though he was not yet sure how he'd do it, he would need to earn their trust one way or the other to get them to talk.

"Oh, um, it's nothing," Debra declared. Daniel could feel her attempting to inconspicuously pull her arm from his grip. As Cassie stared wide-eyed at Debra's bandage, Daniel dared not relinquish it.

"May I?" he asked politely pointing to the wrap. Once Debra shakily nodded, Daniel began to unwrap the bandage. He intentionally untangled it slowly in a sloth-like motion. The room was silent until he finished, and when he finally spotted the bruising on her wrist, he looked up at her, shaking his head. "My dear, this is not nothing! Please, tell me you will let me arrange for my people to look at this at some point. I insist."

"I guess that would be all right," Debra sighed. She looked from him back down to her hand with sad eyes like those of a puppy.

"Great then!" Daniel smiled wide for a moment or two before he proceeded to re-wrap Debra's arm. When he finished, he gave it two soft pats before he finally let it fall slowly back to her side. "Might I sit ladies?"

"Yes, of course," Cassie said, the bright red hue coloring her face slowly fading now that he'd released Debra's arm.

He turned right back to Cassie as he hummed, "Oh, and thank you very much for this, my dear. I'm quite parched, indeed." Cassie nodded, sat down with the others at the table, and then there was a brief silence while Daniel scanned the sisters. He truthfully found their messy, freckled appearance to be kind of interesting. "So!" he shouted suddenly, "Back to the purpose of my being here. It's been my intention since arriving to get to know each member of this town and to truly understand how it is we can make all of y'all's lives better. So first of all, please accept my apologies for all the ruckus that's come with us thus far. We didn't expect our men to run into the resistance that they did at the Morrell home, and the use of force was the last thing we wanted—especially of a lethal nature!"

Cassie and Debra exchanged a quick look before finally replying.

"I'm sorry," Debra replied leaning forward. "What do you mean by resistance?"

"Well, the Morrells shot at our men first at that house, and unfortunately, they were forced to take action in self-defense," he answered. "It's a shame. From what I heard they were good people."

Cassie looked down and uttered solemnly, "They were very good people, yes."

"Well, their loss will not be forgotten," Daniel blurted, nearly interrupting her. "Now where was I? Oh yes, bringing order and safe commerce to the Riverlands. So far, I've begun working on this mission of mine by going home to home to determine the needs and abilities of each person. That's what brings me here to you this morning, but is not the only reason I am here. I had a conversation today with a man who I might describe as a curious character. Actually, curious wouldn't do him justice. I think I would rather use the word simple. Very simple."

"You're talking about Charles Langston, aren't you?" Debra asked sharply. "That man is delusional. He thinks he's the mayor of Harran, you know?"

Daniel burst into a loud, exaggerated laughter. "Yes, that's the man!" he replied with a cackle. Then, in an instant, he went stern. At this point he was just having fun with this game he was playing. These conversations were some of his favorite moments in life. "However, despite his foolishness, he had some interesting things to say about y'all. Supposedly, he believes that y'all have something you might be trying to hide. Might this claim have any validity?" he asked, as the sisters sat frozen.

"Of course not," Debra declared. "Charles Langston is an idiot. It's a wonder that man has even survived for as long as he has here in the Murrieta. As a matter of fact, if there's anyone in this town I would be skeptical of, it would be him for exactly that reason.

He actually claims to have political ties to the East that justify his position here. Now am I saying that's the least bit believable based on his word? Obviously not. But I truly can't think of any other way he could even be alive."

"Well that would certainly be an unexpected scenario, now wouldn't it?" Daniel chimed.

". . . And perhaps that's exactly what his game is," Cassie added.

"Perhaps indeed," Daniel nodded, impressed by the dynamic of how Cassie and Debra seemed to build off each other. "Well I appreciate hearing y'all's perspective on things. I can see I'll have to do some more digging in order to get a better understanding of the stories that are being told. I do promise, though, that my investigation will be fair above all else. Despite what you may or may not think of my family, I'm a very understanding man. If you're truthful and open with me, then I will not only show you mercy, but I'll also show you kindness. Now with that being said, I must tell you that if you're not, then I'll show you no mercy and no kindness. I'm not a violent man myself, but if you lie to me, I'll introduce you directly to my brother Clovis. Did you have the chance to meet him when he first led our men into Harran?"

"No, we did not," Debra whispered coldly.

"Well your friends the Morrells did," Daniel quipped. "As a matter of fact, they also crossed him, as I mentioned to you, and we both know what happened to them. You see, we knew Clovis had issues from a young age. By the time we reached our young adult years, our father didn't pay much mind to any of us, but Clovis was treated like a sick dog even as a child. He was a boy who conducted experiments on animals and said things that anyone who didn't know him simply would not understand. My parents didn't know how to deal with this at all, so my brother William and I always tried our best to help him. We struggled with it for a long time, but then we found a home for him when we began our journey into the Murrieta. Clovis thrives in the chaos of this place."

Daniel doubted that they needed to hear more, but he continued anyway, "When we first arrived, there was the matter of finding ourselves a location to serve as a base. William and I decided that strategically the perfect place was Fayette. The only problem was that there was a gang already holding that town, as there were many scattered gangs around the Murrieta. Finding men to back us was not a problem for me, but military strategy wasn't my specialty. Enter Clovis. He immediately rose to the task and guided a massively successful raid. Taking Fayette didn't satisfy him though. Clovis rounded up surviving members of the gang and slaughtered them. There were some that were burned alive, that had their flesh ripped from their bones, and that were mutilated one limb at a time. It was the most ghastly thing I'd ever seen."

Daniel had a difficult time even thinking of the things he had seen at the hands of his brother, let alone speaking of them. The sights would haunt him for the rest of his days, and as he told the story to the Kennedales, he was ever conscious not to show the resulting emotions that welled up inside him.

"But William and I realized that's exactly what we would need here when necessary," he finished with an audible cracking of his voice, "I know y'all's purpose is to do what's in the best interest of each other and y'all's town. I can see it in everything y'all do, and I want to help y'all get what you're after. But I need truth for that to happen. Do y'all understand that?"

The sisters looked down, and Daniel noticed Cassie's eye began to twitch. "We understand," she muttered.

Daniel could see he had her. "There's something y'all ain't telling me, isn't there?"

"Yes," Cassie whispered. Daniel shot upright in his seat, somewhat surprised that his speech had so effectively yielded a result, while Debra sent a mortified look toward her sister. "We know why Charles is so worried about us," Cassie said. "We were afraid to tell you, and as difficult as he is to deal with, he is a member of our town. You have to forgive us, we simply knew him better than we knew you, and he also threatened us."

"I assure you," Daniel beamed, "Y'all won't be retaliated against for providing information to me. We will not let him hurt you."

"All right," Cassie whimpered as she looked to Debra. "If we have his word, then we have to tell him. This is a new time for Harran, and we need to adapt to it, sister."

"I understand," Debra muttered after a slight hesitation. "I trust you, Cassie."

Cassie nodded and turned back to Daniel. "Last night we had an argument with one of your men that really shook us up," she began. "It's the real reason Debra's arm is wrapped up. Anyway, after we got her arm taken care of, we decided to take a walk through town to cool off. While walking, we noticed someone who had come out of the saloon appeared to be insulting Charles. He was ridiculing him fiercely, and Charles is a sensitive man, as you can probably imagine."

"Oh believe me, I noticed that rather quickly," Daniel chuckled.

"I thought you might," Cassie complimented him, as Debra now sat tall in her chair. "You seem to have a great ability to see who people are at their core." An ear-to-ear smile then crossed Debra's face, which made Daniel feel better about where they stood. Perhaps their fear had fostered a type of trust in him. "As I was saying though," Cassie continued, "the man was insulting Charles harshly about how he wasn't actually the mayor of anything and has no authority and such. The man was very drunk and inevitably the tension led to an altercation." Cassie paused, looking Daniel dead in the eye. "Now Charles might be dumb, but he is not weak, and when he's angry he's a force to be reckoned with. Charles rapidly overpowered your man and in a fit of rage drove the man's own hunting knife into his face. Unfortunately for us, we saw the whole thing. Once the deed was done he was covered in blood and made us swear not to tell anyone. He threatened us multiple times, so we gave him our word and scurried off. We did keep an eye on him though from a distance and saw him drag the body off into the woods." Cassie stopped and Debra reached over and gave her sister's hand a squeeze.

"I'd like to first say that I believe y'all are being sincere with me, and I can tell you are shaken by what you had seen," Daniel exhaled, overwhelmed by the story. "However, I cannot yet take action to detain him unless I have some form of proof. Might you be able to lead us to an approximate location of the body?"

"We should be able to do that, yes," Debra confirmed. "As Cassie said, we have a pretty good idea of its location."

Suddenly, another knock came to the Kennedale door. Debra rose and answered it again. Daniel noticed it was two of his men, so he walked outside to talk to them. After they gave him a quick briefing about a guard who was left unconscious, which frankly he thought was a pain in the ass to handle considering the fun he'd been having here, he thanked them and came back in to the sisters.

"I would like to thank you ladies again for your assistance," he offered kindly. "I'll return shortly so that we may investigate this senseless murder. For now though, I must respond to another matter. It appears one of our guards was left unconscious earlier in the morning. This is certainly an interesting little place y'all live in!"

With that, Daniel Keagan left the Kennedales, who were standing still and silent, behind him. He could not believe all the excitement that this town afforded, but his role as its overseer was the type of thrill he lived for. To him, it was only a matter of time before he'd take it one step further and become its full-fledged puppet master.

Daniel then followed his men toward the post of the guard who had been knocked out that morning. The fellow was sitting on the ground with his arms around his knees. He appeared dazed at first, but he immediately came to and stood at attention when he spotted Daniel Keagan coming his way.

"Please, let yourself be at ease," Daniel encouraged the guard as he approached. "I'm sorry, but please remind me of your name. I've met too many people to keep track of since arriving here and I'm not entirely familiar with all of Clovis's men."

"Not to worry, sir," the man assured him. "My name is Collin McCormack. I apologize for letting myself be taken down earlier. I assure you it won't happen again."

Daniel rested a hand on Collin's shoulder and assured him, "You have nothing to apologize for, Collin McCormack. Just please tell me what happened here, so that I can figure out how to remedy the situation."

Collin nodded and explained, "Well, I was needed out on guard duty last night after a stint at the saloon, so as you can imagine by the morning I was very tired. During my time in the saloon, there was this magician man. I believe his name was Nicholas. He was talented and did tricks for everyone in the place. He also told us he had a show to do in some town a little further west. Come to think of it, he never did mention the name of the town . . . Anyway, this morning he approached my post with a horse and trailer to go to his show, so I somewhat let my guard down since I remembered him."

"Were you able to see what was in the trailer?" Daniel asked.

"See that's the thing," Collin replied with a trace of shame. "I told him I'd need to search it first, I swear on my life I did! But then he quickly changed the subject and did a trick that he used to distract me. Once my attention was taken, he knocked me out. The trailer was covered, too, so I never did get any kind of look inside it."

"I understand. Don't let it trouble you," Daniel replied. "I believe that you did all you could under the circumstances. This Nicholas fellow was clearly hiding something, and we need to find out what it is. Thank you for your assistance, Collin. If you'll please excuse me, I must figure out how we'll find this man."

"You're welcome, sir. I thank you as well for your understanding. It isn't something I'm as accustomed to being under Clovis. With his being such a great, stern leader, I mean, of course. But please wait," Collin pleaded. "As for Nicholas, he shouldn't be hard to track with his horse and trailer. If you're planning to send men to go after him then you must let me go, too. I beg of you. That scumbag illusionist insulted me, and on my honor I cannot let him get away with it."

Daniel was pleased with Collin's determination. He paused for a brief moment in thought. "All right, that seems like a good plan," he said as he turned to the two messengers. "You two go with Collin and track this man down." After they agreed, he turned back to Collin. "Now I need you, sir, to listen to my instructions clearly, because what I'm about to tell you is straight from my brother Billy. Do you understand?"

"Yes, sir," Collin promised. "I understand completely."

"Good. Now, when you find Nicholas it would be preferable to ensure that he's returned to us alive," Daniel explained. "I've received word from my brother that Jeannie Morrell escaped, and the last she was seen was here in the Riverlands at a V'ahani camp. Because of this, I'm considering any abnormal activity from the people of Harran to be suspect. If you see that she does happen to be with this man once captured, then do what you must to subdue him, but you don't dare lay a goddamn finger on her, do you understand me?"

"Absolutely," Collin stuttered, now breathing heavily. "I definitely appreciate your confidence in me to assign this task, and I won't let you down."

"I know you won't," Daniel confirmed. "I must be off now, and so should you. They have a few hours advantage on you, so there's no need for me to say this but be sure to make haste."

Collin nodded confidently and went with the two men to round up horses and weapons. Daniel then made his way back to the Kennedales' house. It had been a very busy morning and exhaustion was creeping in, but he wouldn't have had it any other way. He liked to think of himself as a person who got things done, and he enthusiastically accepted the challenge.

After his brief walk through town, he arrived and knocked on the door. Debra's face was on the other side again as it cracked open. "Show me," he said coldly.

The sisters got their things and led him toward a wooded area. As they walked through the lightly snow-covered ground, Daniel noticed they were shaking. He respected their bravery to do this despite their fear of the alleged violence of Charles Langston. The sisters turned to him after a short time, and Debra explained that they believed the point to be halfway between Charles's home and that of the next house over. They would need to measure that point now.

Once they did, Cassie turned to him and muttered, "This way."

Under her breath, Daniel could hear Cassie counting her paces. As her count rose, she moved progressively slower. Daniel could sense a kind of doubt and fear in her, which put him on edge. "Thirty . . ." she whispered. "Thirty five . . . Forty . . . Forty-five . . ."

Suddenly Cassie stopped counting. Daniel glanced around and noticed that a thick wooden tree branch was sticking out from the ground and jutting awkwardly into the air. Cassie trotted over to it.

"This looks right," she called to her sister.

It didn't take extensive digging to find the body. It wasn't buried deep—just deep enough to have remained unseen. Daniel decided it was enough once he saw the face. He looked to the sisters, who now had his trust.

"So you say this occurred outside the saloon?"

"Yes, somewhere around there," Debra replied.

"Very well, I'll go to his home with some men," he said. "This should all be over shortly. I appreciate your assistance in this matter. Know that you're safe here in Harran, and I look forward to providing you with the same livelihood you enjoyed before." The sisters nodded at him and remained in place. As Daniel made his way out of the woods, he looked back to see them staring at each other. Odd sisters, certainly, but trustworthy, for now.

Shortly after, he rounded up a group of men and made his way over to the home of Charles Langston. His armed followers stayed out of sight as Daniel came to the door. In an instant, his knock was answered.

"Daniel," Charles yelped, "What can I do for you?"

"Hello, Charles," Daniel greeted. "If you could let me in, I simply have a question or two to ask you."

"Of course, come right on in!" Charles exclaimed.

They sat down at the table, and Daniel began, "As I said this should be very brief. Charles, did you pass by the saloon at any time last evening?"

Charles stared at the ceiling for a second. "Um, yes I did. I don't drink though, and I was just passing by. I like to keep an eye on the folks that go in and out of there to make sure no one's causing any trouble, you see."

"I see," Daniel exhaled. "And last night, did you happen to notice anyone walking out of the place who was causing trouble?"

Charles paused for a moment again and played with the scant hair on the sides of his head before answering, "I did see a man walking out who was very intoxicated, yes. I greeted him briefly to see precisely how intoxicated on my way to return home. He was fairly along and not a very friendly fellow, but seemed fine enough, so I left."

This was enough evidence for Daniel. "Thanks, Charles," he said feeling pleased with his detective skills. Then, he walked briskly over to the door and knocked on it two times. His men rushed inside to detain Charles.

The large, boorish man became irate when he was taken hold of and began screaming in a fit of rage. "What's the meaning of this!?" he shouted.

"You're being apprehended for the murder of a member of the Keagan Gang," Daniel declared. "Eventually you'll be brought before my brother Billy, and he'll decide how you're to be punished."

Charles fought and wailed at the top of his lungs as he was dragged out of his home. The people of Harran emerged to the streets to behold the commotion. As the "mayor" of the town, Daniel could tell it was unbearable for him to be seen this way by its inhabitants. In some way, he almost felt pity for the man. Then Charles was walked past the Kennedale sisters, who were grinning in his direction. Cassie lifted a hand and gently waved to him.

With just the wave, he became twice as maniacal. "You don't have a fucking clue what I'm capable of!" Charles shouted at the top of his lungs. He looked directly at them and promised, "You bitches will pay for this! You'll all pay for this! The people I know will destroy this entire God forsaken place if any harm whatsoever befalls me!"

Charles carried on this way until he was taken out of sight.

Once he was, Daniel walked over to Cassie and Debra and quipped, "For all of our sakes, I sure hope his claims really are just foolishness, huh?" With that lunatic gone and having had the amusing opportunity to play detective, Daniel was ready to focus more directly on establishing the relationships that would help the Keagans own the North—and he now knew exactly where to start.

CHAPTER 7

WHAT ONCE WAS WHOLE

Harran was now out of sight, and there was no more need to hide. Jeannie felt nothing but relief to be out of the now Keagan-infested town. As they progressed north along the River White, she noticed it had become quite calm, and she could now see through it a little more clearly. For the first time, its rushing water seemed to flow smoothly over the rocky riverbed, rather than continuously crashing down onto it.

Though Jeannie remained in the trailer with Hanzah, she eavesdropped intently on Harrison and Dominic, who were walking slightly ahead with Nala.

"My father never allowed me to travel as far north as the Mountainlands with him," Harrison said. "He always told me it was too dangerous for someone my age."

"Yes, I'm sure he was right about that," Dominic replied. "I wouldn't say too dangerous for someone your age as much as it's dangerous for anyone. The peril of the journey is what makes the services your dad offered so valuable to the people of the East. The Mountainlands contain many riches. His relationships and skills allowed us to thrive here, sharing in those riches and offering the natives our own."

Jeannie inhaled the praise bestowed upon her father.

"So how will we make it there on our own?" Harrison asked.

Dominic gestured to Hanzah and responded, "That's a question better suited for our V'ahani guide." Jeannie could feel Hanzah sit up a little straighter next to her.

"Well," Hanzah began to explain, "we must continue to follow the River White north until it leads us to the mountains. The problem is that a branch of the river flows alongside the length of the mountain range, so we must cross it to get to the safest path through. There is a manmade bridge crafted by my people that can be used for this, but it is old and, at this time of year, the water is likely to be thinly frozen that far north. It is not a path commonly traveled in the winter."

"So once we cross the river will we be traveling safely for the rest of the way?" Harrison asked.

"My apologies, but when I said 'safest path' I misspoke," Hanzah muttered regrettably. "There is no safe route through the mountains by any means. One issue is that the grizzlies are not as prevalent in those parts so we will have only our pistols for defense prior to reaching the camp of my uncle. The winter weather is also unkind when coupled with the steepness of the icy hills. Really, the only benefits of the path we seek are that it is the closest thing to a flat trail and will guide us in the direction we need to go. Once we make it through, my people will be located in the valley on the other side."

Dominic chuckled. "See my friends?" he said, turning to the Morrells. "No reason to worry!"

Despite Dominic's playfulness, Jeannie found many reasons to worry based on Hanzah's description. She began to swing her legs, which were hanging over the trailer, in thought.

"Look," Hanzah followed, "I appreciate you all feeling like you owe me something, but if this journey presents you with a risk that is not worth taking then please know you can turn around right now. I would not hold it against you if you decided to leave and go back east. That would certainly be the safest option."

Jeannie scoffed at this notion. "Harrison and I aren't ever going back east," she declared. "The Murrieta is our home now so this is the only way. We need you and your people as much as you need us."

"She's right," Harrison agreed. "We'll make it through at all costs. It would be far worse for us to live with ourselves if we gave up now."

"This is good to hear," Hanzah replied. "It is difficult for me to imagine that I would be able to make it without you all. For now, we should continue on until we reach the branch in the River White where the mountains begin. Once we do, we can make camp while we plan out our way across."

"Sounds good to me," Dominic called.

As they continued on along the river Jeannie began to wonder when the crashing of the current would resume.

*

Day turned to night and then came back again like the flip of a coin. Following the Keagan raid, the V'ahani of the Riverlands pressed on.

Latera was watching the rations. They were growing smaller

and smaller with each meal. There was so little to go around that two of the horses could not make it any further and eventually died of exhaustion. Though there remained a gleaming beauty to the rocky hills they passed, Latera only felt deceived by their eminence. With the lack of food to survive on and the conditions of winter remaining, it was too painful for her to admire anything as she saw her people suffer.

What made things even harder, though, was Elan's sudden "absence" as Latera had come to think of it. He was present in body but not in any other significant way. Prior to the raid, he had been so supportive and helpful in guiding and encouraging her people. Yet as the reality of the situation started to sink in, his attitude had dramatically worsened. Latera found herself hurt by the fact that he was so fair weather in his conviction of their success, especially after his strange outburst when he saved her. The distance he purposely wedged between them stung, too, when considering the bond that had been developing between them previously. Something was not right—something bothered him beyond the hard times her people had come upon. But he would hardly speak to her at all, let alone tell her what it was. Now on her own to encourage the rapidly crumbling spirit of the V'ahani men and women, Latera realized that she would need to rely on herself alone for strength. This would be quite the challenge, too, since physically, she hardly had any left, and emotionally, only her fury at her father's murderers remained.

Just as she began to lose feeling in her legs, and as if in an answer to her silent prayer, Lennox suddenly shouted. "A camp! A camp!"

Through the snowfall, Latera could not make out if anyone was inside the small gathering of pitched tents, but she could see the camp itself.

"That's the Tokali," Elan exerted, a rare bit of excitement in his voice. With his confirmation, the V'ahani rushed the camp, paying no mind to who awaited inside. Fortunately, the camp was abandoned. Not a soul even gave this a second thought, though, as a mad search for any form of sustenance commenced. Wails of joy could be heard throughout as fair amounts of vegetables, hunted carcasses, and soup were found.

"Please!" Lennox desperately shouted to no avail. "We must preserve some for the remainder of the road ahead!"

Replies of discontent rang out, "What we must do is eat! It's your fault we are in this mess in the first place!"

Latera found she was pleased that sentiment was starting to swing out of favor of the councilmen. It made her confident that she would have the support of the others when it became time to seek justice. Though Lennox's plea had reason, Latera knew that nothing he did would be able to stop the people from eating until their bellies were full. They had been empty too long to quell the hunger now. Appearing defeated, the councilmen too soon made their own attempts to scrounge for whatever bites they could get. After they satisfied their own stomachs, they made their way over to Castor, who was sitting completely still on his own. Latera, having now found something to hold her over, found a place covertly close by to sit and spy on them.

With some of their meal remaining, they walked slowly over to him. He didn't even turn as they approached him. As Latera observed Castor, she noticed how hollow he looked, but she felt no pity. Maybe now he understood the gravity of what he had done. Parish placed a hand on his arm and still he did not move a muscle. "You need to eat something Castor," Parish pleaded. "Here, finish the rest of ours."

Finally, Castor turned to the two men. "Can I tell the two of you something?"

Lennox and Parish exchanged stressed looks.

"Yes, what is it?" Lennox asked.

"One evening when I was a younger man," Castor whispered, "my father and I went out hunting closer to the mountains. We sat camped out in a brush for some time and eventually saw a passing wolf pack."

"Is this going to go somewhere?" Parish asked.

Without any pause or reaction to the interruption, Castor continued. "Not long after they emerged though, another pack reared their heads a little too close by. The first group of wolves didn't like this obviously, as the second was trespassing on their territory. Then the intimidation tactics began. My father could tell awfully quickly which two wolves were the respective alphas. 'Those two are calling the shots' he told me, pointing them out. 'No doubt about it.' Then, he looked upon the wolves in shame because he knew what was coming next. After some more growling and carrying on, sure enough they charged at each other."

Parish suddenly got up and stormed off.

"Where are you—," Lennox began, but Castor still continued.

"Needless to say, not many survived this battle, and the two alphas were actually the first ones to go. Those that did survive limped off and hardly maintained the strength to do so. When they had all gone, my father looked at me and you know what he said?" Lennox, now glaring at him blankly, shook his head. "He told me that what I had just seen was justice, but it was justice only because the alphas had died. They attempted to achieve something positive for their respective packs but had put those they were meant to protect in danger in order to do so and therefore they deserved the consequences. 'Now do not get me wrong,' he said to me. 'They are animals and they lack the ability to understand the concept of peaceful resolution, which is what separates us from them. However, some men, weak men, still attempt to accomplish things in the same way as these wolves.'"

"I can see how you might see us as the wolves, Castor, but—,"

"The last thing he said though has been stuck in my head ever since. It rings like bells, both when I sleep and when I am awake. What he said was, 'No matter the outcome, even if every member of the pack had survived, as people who have the ability to communicate it is our duty to do so in the face of conflict. Unfortunately, there are far more of us in this world that fail to understand that than those that grasp it. So often we are no better than the wolves. But you son, you must be better.'" Finally showing some emotion, Castor began to well up and shrieked at Lennox, "It is as if I have learned nothing! Like every lesson that has come my way has been wasted!"

"Well maybe you have," Lennox replied angrily, seemingly giving up on getting through to Castor, at least initially. "Even if a wrong decision was made though, we can only correct it by trying our best to now do what is right. Can you not see that?"

Castor stared at him without a word and scoffed. Within an

instant though, his expression once again seemed to fade away. "It is too late for that," he whispered. "It is far too late."

It was in that moment that Latera could see the councilman had become a man without a name—a person who had accepted his fate and become nothing. Castor was now gone, and as Lennox finally turned away from the figure that sat in his place, she wondered if anyone would be safe from whoever it was that remained.

Once the councilmen were all departed, Latera left her spot to see if she could find more food. It wasn't pleasant, this desperation. It was magnified by how messy she felt. Since arriving at this camp, she'd let her hair fall loose, and though it was somewhat freeing, she had always been accustomed to it being held together to some degree. Brought back to her hunger, she eventually came to a tent that seemed to be empty. When she entered however, she heard someone jump inside. She became on edge over the aggressive action, but her stomach dropped when she saw that it was Elan.

"Are you going to stay and talk to me?" she asked coldly after an initial period of silence. "Or are you going to scurry off and continue to avoid me? I know that is what you are doing, Elan."

He carried on with his search for food. "I am not purposely avoiding you, Latera," he exhaled. "I know I have not been helping you lately. Ever since what happened, I am just worried and hungry like everyone else. The thought that after my whole journey I might not make it back to the people counting on me is horrifying—it has kept me preoccupied. And I am sorry."

She felt her compassion stir, realizing that they shared a similar weight of responsibility to their people, and she tried to comfort him. "That makes sense to me, and I cannot fault you for that, but you must be honest with me and tell me that up front then," she pleaded. "I am carrying the weight of boosting morale on my own, and this is a journey you asked us to make. It hurts to see you lose faith in it." She paused. "And I have missed your friendship."

"Friendship?" he started. "No, I am not your friend, Latera. I am least of all that."

He scratched his head a moment and then finally addressed her.

"For the sake of the Mother! Can you not sense I have feelings for you? I have wanted to tell you—"

"Elan—"

"No! Let me finish this piece. I take it back. I may have had feelings for you, but they are senseless. We could never be together, and that is all that matters. Before this moment, I did not know how to be honest with myself about it—let alone with you," he declared. "I placed distance between us to quiet my own feelings. Our people . . . they are just too different. Though we want to unite as tribes, my family and friends wouldn't look favorably upon a relationship between us. Who knows, maybe my lack of spine in this means I never truly cared for you at all. I probably never did and never will. Or . . . maybe . . . who knows. It does not matter. All I know is there would only be hurt down the path for us. I think I am beginning to realize that this whole journey—everything about it—is more complicated and challenging than I thought."

Latera paused, digesting his words. "I was beginning to like you too, Elan, but . . ." she took a breath, "we can just be friends—we can just be the allies our people plan to be, and I have no problem with that. If you need time to distance yourself from any other feelings, I understand, but just say that to me.

There is no need for dishonesty here."

"No dishonesty, you say? Well then. Yes, we are allies, Latera," Elan murmured. "But we are nothing more than that. We can be nothing more than that. We cannot even be friends."

At this, Latera felt the pain and anger pour into her. She'd already lost so much, and now she couldn't even keep her only remaining friend on this journey? Why couldn't Elan maintain their friendship? The other feelings were new and young, and they could be put to rest. She agreed to lay them aside. Why couldn't he? She needed a friend more than a lover right now, and their friendship had been the strongest aspect of their relationship. The trust they'd formed—that was precious in these treacherous times. Latera could see that Elan didn't want to have to say the things he did. There was no hiding that. But whatever it was he had truly felt though, it didn't matter—not if this was his final decision.

"You know, you really are no hero," she sharply replied. "You made this journey thinking you would become one, but what have you really become besides lost, Elan? A hero puts the needs of others before his own, and now things have gotten hard, and all you have done is buckle. Do you even realize what I have been through? I lost my father and I thought I lost my brother. Though guess what? Turns out my brother is actually alive! Turns out he escaped the wrath of the same gutless councilmen who betrayed our father and their own leader and then lied to our people! My brother lives! Yet even though I am apart from him—apart from the only family I have left—I put my people first, even if it means quietly following the despicable men that murdered my father to do so." Elan was speechless and his mouth dropped wide open at this revelation. "But please, take your time to get over your feelings and confusion. As for me, I will make sure we survive with or without you and your Easterner attitude. 'For the sake of the Mother' you have the nerve to say to me? You know nothing of the Mother. You would be as damned in her eyes as you are in mine. Now excuse me, I have a camp of people who I need to go stand up for because no one else will."

With that she exited the tent as quickly as she could and left Elan behind, standing frozen in his place. As she stormed off, initially intending to find her own shelter, she was shocked but empowered by the fire she found inside her. Her path ultimately led her out of the campsite entirely, where she came to the base of a rocky hill. Though it was steep and did not provide a clear path of footing, Latera climbed it. Several times she slipped on the smooth but dirty rocks, acquiring bumps and bruises on the way up. The more she fell, the more calculated her next maneuvers around the stair-like edges became. After completing the mazelike climb, she finally reached the top. Before her stood the massive landscape they'd left behind them, the path of their journey now carved into it. Rolling hills that told the story of her travels thus far were blanketed in trees and a layer of snow. Though the scope of her vision was finite, the emotions and weight of her frame were endless. Latera now stood above it all. There on her perch she was higher than the Riverlands, higher than the councilmen, higher than Elan and all those who had wronged her thus far. Then, peering down at the marks she had made on her way up, she smiled. She hadn't received these new scars; she'd earned them. If she only kept climbing higher, the smaller everything and everyone below her would look.

After days of trekking north along the River White, Dominic and his troupe had finally reached the branch of the river they'd need to cross over to get to the mountains. The camp they made once they arrived sat at the beginning of an open field, which looked out on the river and mountains. As light began to fill the sky, Dominic admired the snow-capped mountain peaks, which did not even look real behind the large, icy river. It was all so majestic and made him feel a great relief at its peacefulness. He thought that maybe this was his reward for having found a better solution in disorienting the guard back in Harran rather than taking his life. As he beheld the scenic view, he brought his hands together, but this time it was only to rub them against one another.

"Eat something, my friends," Dominic urged. He passed the children cooked squirrels, which he had hunted earlier in the morning. "You'll need your strength for what's to come."

They all grabbed their share and dug in. At one point, Harrison looked up from his meal and toward the river.

"Should we come up with a strategy?" he asked.

"A strategy for what?" Dominic replied.

"Well, there are four of us, as well as a horse and trailer with a fair stock of supplies in it. So shouldn't we determine a strategy for getting across that bridge?" Harrison answered as he gestured at the size of their group.

It was a good point, Dominic thought.

Yet Hanzah, the most familiar with his people's bridge and crossing it, responded first. "Yes, we should cross one at a time.

Periodically the V'ahani would work to repair the bridge; however, it has been some time since the last repair, as we do not do so in the winter months. We typically avoid the trip altogether at this time of year, so there would be no use repairing it at the end of autumn."

"Good to hear!" Dominic joked, trying to make light of the perilous situation. He believed that humor made every challenge easier to bear, as much as he could tell Hanzah did not get the jokes about his language barrier as much as Jeannie and Harrison did. "We'll go one at a time then until we've all crossed. The biggest challenge will be getting the horse and carriage across. As for the supplies, we can remove them and carry them by hand. I'm not sure that we'd be able to handle the journey physically if we had to carry the supplies all the way through the mountains, so the carriage will be necessary. Also, and I hate to say this, but in the interest of making it with the least amount of weight on the bridge, our best bet might be to have Jeannie lead Nala over."

"Absolutely not!" Harrison shouted. "I nearly lost my sister already, and I won't knowingly put her in harm's way."

"Believe me," Dominic pleaded, hating to always have to be the bearer of difficult news. "I'd never wish to do so either, but it could be the only way."

"Like I said before," Hanzah said, "this journey was mine to make. If there is anyone who should guide the horse across, it should be me."

"That's very fair and honorable of y—" Harrison started to commend the boy, though Dominic had his doubts.

"No," Jeannie interrupted as she looked to her brother. "It's too dangerous for him. I'm by far the lightest. Look, Harrison, I know you want to keep me safe, but safety isn't a luxury we've enjoyed for some time now. Things won't get any easier and this won't be the last time I'll be forced into a situation for our survival."

Dominic found himself repeatedly impressed by little Jeannie's bravery.

"No way," Harrison sighed. "You're very brave, Jeannie, but I can't have this while your safety is my responsibility. I won't let anything happen to you. Not again."

"I believe the bridge should hold if we do it this way, Harrison," Dominic assured him. "But like you said, we won't let anything happen to her under any circumstances."

"Again, I'm her guardian, not you," Harrison angrily replied. "Despite what you've done for her, she also told me about the incident with the knives, and I can't just allow her to be in a situation where she can be harmed."

"Harrison, stop it!" Jeannie shouted. "There is no avoiding danger for any of us, and you aren't the boss of me, even with mother and father gone! I'm crossing that bridge with the load because it's what needs to happen for us to continue on, and we sure as hellfire are gonna continue on."

"The stubbornness of this girl . . ." Harrison jested to the others as he pointed at her. Dominic chuckled as their sibling testiness came out. "Fine, you can go but only once I've determined if it's safe." Just as Jeannie was about to object, Harrison stopped her with a hand in the air, "That's as much crap as I'm gonna take about it and as much ground as I'm gonna cede."

"All right . . ." Dominic started once he believed that they were through. "Now if you're all finished with your meals, we should gather our things and go."

And so they did. Once all of their camping supplies were placed into the carriage, they began their march across the open field toward the river. Dominic couldn't help but look back at the edge of the wooded area where their camp had been. He dreamt of a day when Harran could be back to the way it was, and it saddened him to be leaving it and the last remnant of the Riverlands behind for a while.

Finally they reached a bank that led to the small cliff over the water. Jeannie nervously crept by him to look over the edge. He noted that the river could not have been more than five feet below where they stood, but he could see that the fall would be the least of their worries.

The layer of ice that covered the river was so thin that he could almost make out the un-frozen water that was flowing beneath. There would be no hope if any of them were to fall in, he thought, they'd be swept under the ice in a moment—which brought him to the next dilemma: the bridge. The wooden bridge that crossed over the ice creaked as the wind blew, and although it was wide enough to accommodate the horse and trailer, its strength was another question. Underneath it, he could see the beams that gave it whatever support it did have, but they provided little comfort. He sighed and noted that the Morrells' faces consisted of all different shades of pale. Hanzah seemed to be the only one confident in the bridge his people had constructed, though he admitted that it was not in its best condition.

"Let's begin unloading," Dominic muttered. The group began taking all of the supplies out of the carriage. Dominic grabbed all of his illusionist wares, as he was the only one with the knowledge of the most efficient way of bundling them for transport. Harrison followed by gathering the food and cooking goods, while Hanzah bagged all the remaining necessities such as clothing and the like.

Once everything had been removed, Jeannie took a deep breath, preparing herself, but Harrison broke her concentration as she exhaled.

"I'm crossing first," he declared, to which the others looked puzzled. "In the off chance that this bridge isn't strong enough to hold whatsoever, I'd much rather it is me that falls in than Jeannie. This way, if I do make it, we can be on both sides to help her as she crosses."

Dominic respected Harrison's drive to protect his sister, though he was not surprised considering that he was Adonis's son.

"That would be wise," Hanzah responded. "Since you are lighter than Jeannie and her load, you should be able to make it and get a grasp on whether her weight will hold."

Harrison gave a nod of approval to Hanzah and Dominic. He then made his way over to Jeannie to give her a hug, but she grumpily refused. Harrison wasn't kidding about her stubbornness, Dominic thought to himself. There was no denying how headstrong she was. Harrison looked down sadly for a moment but then continued on toward the bridge.

"The first step is always the greatest obstacle, Harrison," Dominic encouraged him. "Once you take it, you'll realize that the matter of doing the rest will no longer he hindered by your doubts."

Harrison took one last breath, looked up, and took the first step out onto the bridge. The creaking got slightly more pronounced as he crept along—the wind was picking up. Though the path was wide enough, his occasional peering below and the wobbling of the planks made it look like he was performing a balancing act on a single beam. With each step, the tension rose. As he got closer to the other side though, Hanzah began cheering him on. Once the danger of the walk became more evident, Dominic noticed Jeannie's attitude changed and she began to cheer as well.

"Only about twenty more paces!" Dominic shouted, aiming to encourage the young man.

Soon enough, those twenty paces were ten, then five, and then zero.

"You did it!" Jeannie shouted with joy across to him.

Harrison lifted a thumb in the air as he knelt down to catch his breath.

"Well?" Dominic called. "What do you think?"

When he arose, Harrison shook his head. "She can't do it with the horse and the carriage," he declared sadly. "We might have no choice but to leave the carriage and string up as much of our supplies for Nala to carry as she can."

This complicated things, but they would deal with one obstacle at a time.

Dominic walked Jeannie over to Nala and put her hand where it needed to be to guide the animal. "You want to hold her here and hold her firmly," he explained. "If you show her you're confident, she'll be confident in you."

"How am I supposed to focus on that when I have this bridge to cross?" she asked.

"Before I ran into your friend Hanzah here I was just about

ready to give up on this place," he recalled to her with a smile. "I was sure that I had no home anymore and that there'd be nothing that was worth coming back to. But when I did meet this boy and found out that you were alive, I found hope. I realized once again that this place was worth fighting for. Who would've thought that two children could've given that to a grown and traveled man like myself? Let me tell you something: neither of you are ordinary. You're both exceptional, and you have no reason to be anything but confident in yourselves, because it's you that keeps everyone's hope alive."

Jeannie looked to Hanzah.

"You can do this," Hanzah encouraged her.

With a deep breath she turned to look out to Harrison. "I'm ready," she said in a determined tone. Just as Dominic had shown her, Jeannie guided the horse as firmly as she could to the bridge.

As she stood there, she looked up to her brother again at the other end.

"You can do this, Jeannie," he encouraged her. "Just walk toward me, one step at a time."

With this last bit of advice, she took the first step. Her pace was extremely slow and careful, but her ability to remain still with the steed in hand amazed Dominic. He and the boys cheered her on as her march across began. Then, from just beyond where they had been camped, a small group of birds rose into the sky.

Dominic looked up toward it, horrified that Jeannie would become distracted. Still staring up in the air, he asked Hanzah frantically, "Can you call to them and get them to fly in the other direction?"

Hanzah was way ahead of him and already on a knee whispering. The birds were still moving closer, though Jeannie had not yet noticed. Hanzah's whispers began to increase in volume and severity, but still the birds came. Dominic was nearly ready to make a diversion attempt of his own, when suddenly he noticed the birds had begun turning around.

"Great job, Hanzah!" he hailed.

The boy's demeanor shifted immediately. "No!" he replied, shaking his head. "It—"

Three shots immediately rang out through the field, and Dominic heard their impact with the tree trunk just above his head. Almost simultaneously came a shriek from Nala. The terrified horse stood up into the air and hastily, but carefully, began trotting to the other side. Jeannie was knocked off her feet and dragged with the screeching horse.

"Jeannie!" Harrison screamed at the top of his lungs. His pistol was still holstered at his side with all of his attention on his sister, who was now cowering and crying under the beast. She had compacted herself into a tight ball to try to protect her head from Nala's hooves as well as the bridge, but her back was hitting every plank with a ferocity as she was dragged along. She appeared too shocked or terrified to let go, but considering that Nala could collapse the bridge at any moment with her careful, but heavy trots, it was likely better that Jeannie attempted to make it across with her.

With the gunshots, the horse's screeching, and the sight of Jeannie, Dominic was in shock. His ears rang from the bullets, which came too close for comfort, even if they were rather inaccurate. Hanzah came running to him and pulled him to cover behind the trailer. Dominic looked out again in despair at Jeannie and Nala. Then, as another round of shots came, one piercing their cover, his rage overtook him. He pulled out his pistol and continuously unloaded it in the direction of the woods. Next to him, Hanzah was whispering fiercely again.

With the continued commotion, Nala began to panic even more. The horse suddenly stopped, paralyzed in the center of the bridge, too afraid to cross but still stepping back and forth erratically. Realizing his chance to act, Harrison feverishly ran onto the bridge to retrieve Jeannie. Just as he approached her, however, Nala rose into the air onto her hind legs and a snap of wood cracked through the air. Half the width of the plank bridge on which the horse stood collapsed underneath its weight. Much to Dominic's dismay, Nala plunged into the ice, which smashed open underneath her weight. Though Jeannie had instinctively let go of the horse, the force of Nala's plummet caused her to stumble forward into the gap of the bridge.

"Harrison, please!" Dominic heard her cry as she fell.

"NO!" Harrison shouted as he lunged toward her. His sister now hung for dear life to the edge of the half-broken planks that the horse had destroyed. Harrison slid to her side as swiftly as he could and grabbed her arms to pull her to safety. "You're gonna be all right, Jeannie," Dominic heard Harrison promise Jeannie as he carried her to the other side. Once there, the siblings found cover, but not before Dominic saw Harrison reaching for his pistol.

Good, he thought. He and Hanzah would be grateful for the help.

After a third round of shots, Dominic and Hanzah could hear roaring and screams. Hanzah stayed in his place as he continued to perform his ritual, but Dominic saw his chance to move. He was too livid to leave it be. The bastards had nearly killed Jeannie, and they had taken Nala from him. He sprinted across the field and soon came upon the location of the gunfire, though now the scene was only the remnants of a vile attack of Hanzah's grizzlies. The weapons and bodies of two men before him lay in a pile on the ground. Their bones were shattered and their flesh torn apart. Dominic accepted violence when it was necessary, but did not enjoy it by any means. Vengeance was something he did enjoy though, and he soaked it in until he suddenly recalled that there were three shots being fired at a time. Before he could react, he was tackled to the ground from behind. The person on top of him furiously rained punches down on his face. He could hear the exhausted man's heavy breathing and could tell he was weakened.

After taking several blows, he began to fight back, recalling his desire for vengeance. Now he could see that his attacker was none other than Collin McCormack, the guard whom he had knocked unconscious.

"But I let you live," Dominic blurted as they wrestled against each other.

"Biggest mistake of your life," Collin exerted. "You thought you could make a fool of me and get away with it? Fat fucking chance." He then delivered a devastating right hook to Dominic's face, knocking him dizzily to the ground.

"I gave you a second chance, then. Why are you doing this?" Dominic answered, lying still on his back. Looking to his right, he noticed a butt of one of the bear-smashed guns was in reach. To distract his attacker he added, "Want to see a trick?"

"You've got some nerve thinking you could pull that shit on me again, dragon boy," Collin coughed, and Dominic shifted his weight closer to the gun, keeping his eyes on the Keagan man. "Maybe you think you're a comedian now, too?" Collin continued, "Well, hey, I got a joke for you."

Then before Dominic could blink, Collin pounced on top of him and wrapped his hands around his throat. For a few seconds Dominic let the man squeeze, easing him into a sense of victory. Then in one fluid movement, he grabbed the weapon and swiftly smashed it twice into Collin's face.

"SON OF A—" Collin screamed as he fell to the ground, clearly struggling to remain conscious. Collin's face was beaten severely to the point that it was almost unrecognizable.

Though he had prevented his attacker from strangling him to death, Dominic had wasted every bit of energy he had left to do so. The beating he'd taken when Collin had initially launched on him was taking its toll. On the verge of losing consciousness himself, Dominic turned and was relieved to see Hanzah running through the field in their direction.

"You know what?" Collin spoke as he managed to rise to his feet. "This was actually pretty fun. In fact, this was more entertainment than I've had since I first came here."

The man was insane, Dominic thought, casting a wary eye at him.

Then Collin smiled. "You and I, we aren't nearly done. I heard those youngsters calling each other's names on that bridge. I look forward to seeing you and those Morrell kids again very soon, Nicholas."

"You've made a mistake here, and you'll be making a bigger one if you try finding me again," Dominic struggled to sit up, rage pumping through him at the threat to the Morrell children. He needed a weapon—two chances were enough. "My name isn't Nicholas either, it's Dominic Turner. Remember that, you piece of—"

Dominic reached for his discarded pistol and raised it to Collin, but the man was gone, scurrying off back from whence he came. Dominic would never make the shot through the trees. He collapsed back on the ground, the immense pain hitting him, just as Hanzah finally came running up to him.

"Are the others all right?" Dominic asked.

"As much as they could be given the circumstances, yes," the boy replied. "But are you? You are covered in blood."

"I'll make it," Dominic said. "I have no other choice."

CHAPTER 8

KETTLE AND WAKE

Daniel was sitting inside the saloon sipping a beer with one hand and scribbling thoughtfully on a notepad he was using to keep track of his progress in Harran with the other. Every few minutes he would look up and eye the barmaid, who he found to be one fine piece of Murrieta tail. Her loose dress teased just enough to make him wonder about the curves underneath, and her wavy hair was a gold with the type of shine that would make a man greedy.

If there was one thing he couldn't fault the town for, it was its women. Although they weren't as proper as those in Fayette, there was something much more exotic and exciting about them. Daniel very much looked forward to being able to take the time to explore his interest a bit more.

As he smoothly swallowed the last of his hoppy ale down his throat, he saw the barmaid slowly approach out of the corner of his eye. There was a purpose in her step.

"I can see you eyeing me from over here, you know, and I can't say that I mind, handsome," she said flirtatiously. "How'd you like to buy me a drink along with your next one?"

Daniel laughed silently. "If I'm not mistaken, I'd say you must've been eyeing me, too, in that case, and I ain't as easy as you might think, my lady," he replied coyly. "Now you're the one who works here, so how about you go fetch them drinks, and I'll maybe accept your advances. Could even pencil you in on this here busy schedule I got . . ."

She smiled and lifted her hand to her chest. "Well, I'll be damned. That's some nerve you got! My name's Johanna, but call me Jo instead of that 'my lady' crap, if you please. I'll be right back with those drinks," she said with a wink.

"Will do, Jo," Daniel smiled back as she skipped back to the bar. Maybe the exploration would start sooner than he thought.

"Daniel," he was suddenly greeted from behind.

Startled, he made no attempt to hide that he didn't recognize the person standing before him when he turned around. Behind this person, whose face was in terrible condition, was an uppity youngster and recent Keagan addition named Frankie Covington. Finally with one last tilt of his head in an attempt to recognize the man, it hit him.

"Collin?" Daniel asked in disbelief. "Is that you? My goodness, what happened out there?"

"Yes, it's me, sir," Collin reported looking down at his feet with his hands in his pockets. "I have very important news to share with you, Daniel."

"I'm sure you do, but please, let us get your face cleaned and bandaged up first," Daniel practically begged.

"Sir, we picked up the trail of the man who knocked me out days ago," Collin explained, ignoring the suggestion. "His name is actually Dominic Turner and he wasn't going west at all. When we caught up to him, he was crossing a bridge into the mountains with a native boy and two others."

"How do you know it was a native boy?" Daniel asked as Johanna returned to place his drink on the table. She had one for herself in her other hand.

"Jo, if you could just give us a few minutes, please. But don't go nowhere far. I ain't nearly done with you."

She nodded and winked again before leaving them to talk. As she went, Daniel watched her the whole way.

". . . He was dressed in white top-to-bottom, and as you can tell, the men you sent me with weren't lucky enough to escape the monstrous bear that little shithead sent after us," Collin continued. "Their horse did have a nasty fall though, which should slow them down a lot, so I was hoping I could get back up there with a few more men to go after them. They won't be able to stop us this time, I promise, sir. I know how to take them down now."

Daniel tapped his fingers on the table for a moment before chiming, "You mentioned two others that they were with?"

"Yes, of course," Collin exhaled. "That's the most important news of all. One of the two was Jeannie Morrell. Lord knows how they found her, and—"

"You're sure it was Jeannie? You're sure she wasn't harmed?" Though at first Daniel figured Collin's exploits had resulted in failure, he was now pleasantly surprised. Jeannie Morrell!

"I'm nearly certain on both counts, sir," Collin quipped, bouncing and swaying on his feet. "But sir, that isn't even the best part."

Daniel was doubtful that there could be anything in the world

Collin McCormack could know that could be more important than Jeannie Morrell's location, but he opted to humor the man a moment. "And what is?"

Collin practically preened. "You see, sir, the second person that was with her was none other than her brother, Harrison Morrell. Of that I'm sure."

"Wait, what?!" Daniel shouted in disbelief. "You're telling me that Harrison Morrell is alive!? How is that possible!?"

"I don't know how, but I promise you that he is most definitely alive!" Collin cheered.

"Well that is the greatest news I've heard in a long time!" Adonis Morrell's oldest son and heir was even more valuable than the youngest Morrell. He'd pave the way even quicker for them in the North, having accompanied his father in trade dealings. Two Morrells—Daniel couldn't believe it. His brain quickly began analyzing how best to handle the news to a Keagan advantage and began writing furiously on his pad again, trying to get his thoughts down. He'd have to get this to Billy, immediately.

"Collin, I have an important request to make of you," he stated, looking up at the battered man. "After you get yourself patched up, I need you to ride south to Fayette and deliver this news to my brother personally. Take Frankie here with you, as well, so that you aren't traveling alone and so he can grow up a bit. I need y'all to tell Billy that as soon as Clovis is finished with the V'ahani, I'll need him up here with me, so we can develop a strategy to continue our expansion north."

Collin's shoulders slumped and eyes rolled like a grumpy child. "But sir, there's still time to catch them now. And baby-sitting

Frankie will only slow me down further. If I just had a few more men I could go north with and find th—"

"No," Daniel interrupted as Frankie glared at Collin. "Without a concrete plan of action, it would be a foolish waste for any of us to travel up into the Mountainlands. You wouldn't catch them, nor would you survive the journey." Wanting to always maintain the support of his followers, he then assured the man, "Look, I understand that this Dominic fellow insulted you, and I know you want your revenge. I can see the fire inside of you. But right now my brothers and I need you to complete this task for us. If you do so successfully, I promise you that I'll personally give you the permission to find and do with this Dominic what you please."

"Will I be allowed some men to search with, sir? When the time comes in your plan?" Collin asked, rather unwisely in Daniel's opinion. Daniel's kindness only went so far, and it was beginning to fade.

"We will see when the time comes, Collin, but we simply cannot afford to risk the lives of any more of our own without a proper plan. That is final."

"All right then, sir," he finally conceded. "I'll bring this news to Mr. William with haste. I won't let you down again."

"Don't worry about it, Collin," Daniel replied. "Just one more thing. Before you go out to fetch your horse and make this trip, please make sure you tend to your wounds. I'm serious, it's pained me to have even had to look at your face in the condition it's in."

Collin nodded. "I will," he muttered. "Let's go, Frankie."

"Thank you for the opportunity, Mr. Keagan," Frankie enthusiastically said to Daniel, who smiled back kindly. As they walked out toward the doors of the saloon he heard the young man tell Collin, "I know where we can get you wrapped up, if you want to follow me, sir."

Daniel wasn't entirely sure, but as the door shut behind them he thought he could hear Collin snidely remark, "Go fuck yourself, Frankie."

Daniel rolled his eyes, leaned back in his chair, and lifted his beer. "Jo!" he called out through the saloon. "Where'd your gorgeous ass get off to? It's time to celebrate!"

*

The outlook for reaching Orrin's camp now seemed very bleak. With Nala gone and the trailer left behind, the group was forced to carry any essentials that they could. Dominic remained stocked with the travel supplies he thought could be helpful along the way, while the others all carried what food they had left wrapped in tent cloth. Beside these things, they had only pistols and the clothes on their backs. Left behind was extra clothing, equipment that was too much to carry, a fair amount of firewood, and several other items considered to be "luxuries" given their current circumstances.

As for their physical condition, the cold provided no relief to anyone—though Dominic thought it might be hitting him the worst. Along with the beating he took to his face, which was covered in cuts and beginning to swell, his ribs took quite a few blows as well. Walking and breathing became a chore, as he hadn't yet had a chance to rest or recover. Despite the discomfort though, the pain did serve as a sort of distraction from his feeling of weakness in his failure to kill Collin. With the struggles he was now facing both inside and out, simply having a chance to meditate made reaching the Mountainlands camp as soon as possible infinitely more desirable.

After the altercation, he and Hanzah had each struggled across the half-destroyed bridge with their respective supplies. On reaching the other side, they then distributed the loads more evenly and left behind what they believed Nala would be carrying. Then they began down the trail, which carved a path between the massive mountains. Strangely, the angle at which they were now facing the peaks made it feel like they were in a different place entirely. Dominic recalled a landscape from before that was so visually pleasing that it seemed at any moment it could be lifted right out of sight. It had been like a canvas that filled one's eyes. However, they were now looking straight up into the heart of the beast. When focusing on the top of the mountain, Dominic felt as if he were transported to it, feeling a sense of falling even while standing safely at the base. Though still a beautiful sight, even its previously aesthetically pleasing characteristics were now rather haunting.

"How will we make it through with so little supplies to take us there?" Jeannie asked as she stood and stared down the path.

"We have no other choice," Hanzah replied, echoing Dominic's earlier sentiment. With that he began his ascent up the trail into the mountains, with the others following closely behind.

As they progressed, the density of trees along the path thickened. Some were white and splintered in all directions, while others had greens and browns that still seemed to have warmth about them. By the smell of the dead wood, lightning had struck here many times before, and it had struck fiercely. The smell came to distract Dominic as he tripped on one of the stones that littered the trail. While he continued on, the thought came to him that a place like this was a true testament to the plight of the earth and its glorious response. Even in the calm and silence, with the snow falling gently, it was so alive. This was a path that was not forged any more easily than it was walked.

They continued along the trail until the sun began to set. By then, the group was exhausted from a whole day of traveling mostly uphill in the snow. The snowfall was also starting to pick up, indicating that their journey would only become more challenging.

"Is it a good idea to stop and rest now?" Harrison asked.

Dominic's heart skipped a happy beat at the suggestion.

"I believe so. We still have another few days of travel," Hanzah answered. "So with the snow falling heavier now, we need to ensure we have the energy to continue tomorrow. Besides, this should be a good stopping point."

"Let's get to work then; this cold is becoming brutal," Dominic said, trying his best to keep the pleading out of his voice.

They worked efficiently in their setup to minimize the time they would have to spend outside of shelter. In fact, they worked so well as a team that without very much communication, each of them contributed in a different and productive way to pitch the tent and stow their belongings. Once finished and inside, the group sat closely huddled in a circle to warm themselves before going to sleep.

"Can I ask you all something?" Hanzah whispered with his teeth chattering.

"Of course you can," Dominic replied.

"Why do you people all have to leave the East to come here?" he started. "I have heard of how large your cities are and that they only continue to grow. If that is the case, why leave? Why must you all come here and terrorize our home?"

Dominic paused and pondered the question, finding it difficult to do so. He assumed by Jeannie's and Harrison's silence that they must find it just as troublesome to answer as he did. The boy certainly didn't mean to lump them in with the Keagans and the other terrible gangs. Did he? "Hmm . . . a very bold question," Dominic finally responded.

"I am not sure I see how it is bold," Hanzah answered.

"Well it's a little unfair to ask of us that question as if we are part of the problem, given we are helping and all," Harrison said.

"Unfair?" Hanzah repeated. "Is it not also unfair that you have your sister here beside you while mine is being led by traitors and stalked by a band of murderers? I may never see her again. I may never see any of my family again. That is what is truly unfair, and if it were not for the greed of you Easterners it would not be that way at all."

"We come because for some of us the big cities grow too tall," Dominic replied, and he recognized Hanzah's expression shift away from anger to inquisition. "In time, they become so vast that it's as if you could get swallowed whole within them. The highrises, the crowded streets, the smell of concrete and of human piss, and shit in the alleyways—it becomes too much. It all used to make me feel so low, and yet when I was there, the city itself was my only friend. I used to try to tell myself it inspired me, but it was all just a lie. And what it came down to was I just wasn't entirely free there. Once a place has grown beyond the scope of a person's ability to comprehend building upon it, I suppose it just loses its meaning. It is lost in the masses."

"And for some, like our father, that can be a good thing," Harrison seemed determined to add.

Hanzah stared idly at the three of them. To Dominic it appeared that Hanzah wanted to understand but just couldn't. Their backgrounds certainly were very different, but they were brought together by greater forces and would need to disregard those differences, not emphasize them, if they were to succeed.

"I think it would be best for me to just get some rest," Hanzah declared as he hunched over to sleep.

The others followed suite soon after, and Dominic slept that night as well as he could have considering how cold it was becoming even inside their tent. When they woke, the clouds remained in the sky, and conditions continued to deteriorate. They traveled along the trail for another day, which, once again, went relatively well. The path was beginning to become icy, and they did have the occasional slip at times, but otherwise their greatest worry was keeping warm.

That evening once they made camp again, they also decided to gather wood to build a fire, which provided great relief. Once again, Dominic rested easy through the night. This time when morning came, he could see the sun rising—the clouds finally dispersed. Once his things were packed, he marveled at the way its rays hugged the cliffs. Though there was a building fog, this morning finally felt pleasant.

Dominic watched as Harrison approached his sister and put his arm around her.

"I wish Donovan could see this," Jeannie said quietly in response.

"He can, sister. I'm sure he can," Harrison replied.

How his heart ached for these surviving Morrells.

Just then, howling filled the air. The group froze at first before racing toward each other and standing in a tightknit formation.

"Hounds?" Jeannie cried. "Oh please don't let it be the hounds again."

"Worse," Hanzah whispered as the sounds grew louder. "Those are wolf calls. By the sound of it . . . a pack. Maybe about four of them or so."

"Can your people not speak to them, Hanzah?" Jeannie asked. "Can you not tell them to pass?"

Dominic had the same thought, hope rising in him, even as the calls grew nearer.

"Unfortunately, we cannot," he regretfully replied. "Wolves cannot be tamed. Our words have no meaning to a hungry wolf. It would be best to prepare your weapons now."

"Damn it," Dominic muttered under his breath, careful not to let the children hear the fear in his voice. He drew his pistol, looking in every direction in anticipation of the coming threat. Sure enough, a pack of five wolves finally emerged from different parts of the foggy tree line. They began to snarl angrily as they stared down the intruders in their territory.

"Should we shoot?" Jeannie whispered, her gun arm shaking.

"Hold on; there are too many," Dominic replied as the beasts made their creeping approach. "By the time we get four shots off, one of them will still be upon us even if we're lucky enough to down the others." His focus never left the pack, which seemed ready to strike.

"So what should we do?" Harrison mumbled.

Dominic's eyes raced around until he landed upon a plan. Out of the corner of his mouth, he answered, "Only when I say 'now' will you shoot. Until then we won't have the advantage. Ready yourselves and aim for the kill."

They waited, but much to Dominic's dismay, Jeannie's shaking hand accidentally fired a shot. The bullet pierced the shoulder of her target. At first there was a whimper, and the wolves paused, but with ferocity they leaped forward into a charge, even the injured wolf joining in the run after a moment.

"NOW!" Dominic shouted, desperately reaching into the pocket of his coat. He and the boys fired their weapons while Jeannie tried to reload. Then Dominic grabbed the smoke bomb from his pocket and threw it straight to the ground in front of him. A shroud of smoke began to cover them.

Jeannie, Harrison, and Hanzah all stopped reloading their weapons and beheld what was occurring around them. Dominic cast a glance around through the smoke; he and the boys had taken their shots from much closer range and hit their targets with kill shots. So now only two wolves remained, including the injured one. Dominic realized that because of the early shot, they would not be completely submerged in smoke fast enough to avoid the remaining attackers outright, as had been his original intention. In a split-second decision, he grabbed the others, pulling them to a knee on the ground and covering them under their thick tent sheet.

"Don't move!" he shouted just as the wolves pounced into the smoke. Fortunately, without visibility the weakened animals landed awkwardly, missing their targets. The injured wolf could be heard whimpering more dramatically now as the final remaining wolf began biting and clawing at the sheet.

"What do we do!?" Harrison yelled.

Activity from inside their cover was frantic as they attempted to fend off the threat.

Then Hanzah let out a horrid scream. The wolf's jaws had bit straight down into his forearm through the sheet. Once it had him, it began heaving back and forth violently, removing the others from the cover. As Dominic emerged from the sheet, the smoke was now so thick that it was impossible to see through, and he soon realized that Hanzah and the wolf were no longer with them. Hanzah's screaming persisted as Dominic, Jeannie, and Harrison crawled feverishly around to find him. In a moment, Jeannie disappeared as well. Harrison looked up at Dominic.

"Jeannie?" Harrison called out. "Jeannie!"

A pistol shot rang out, silencing all the yelling and snarling, and Dominic felt his stomach bottom out. When the smoke had finally cleared, he saw Jeannie kneeling over Hanzah. Dominic beheld the sight of the slain wolves and felt himself quaking from the inside out. The trauma was beginning to take a toll. Once he collected himself he looked toward the others. Harrison had run over to his sister and was kneeling next to her.

"I'm sorry!" Jeannie shouted as tears poured from her eyes. "It's all my fault! I'm so sorry!"

Dominic could not see Hanzah from his position behind

Jeannie, so he rushed over and gently nudged her aside. There on the ground the bloodied Hanzah lay completely still. His contorted forearm was badly broken, which made Dominic suck in a breath and, for the first time in a long time, pray.

*

The V'ahani had finally exhausted all of the available food that they had been left at the abandoned Tokali camp and were now preparing to continue traveling toward the Hold. Latera avoided eye contact with Elan completely since their confrontation. It continued to frustrate her a great deal that he could so quickly shy away from the trust and friendship they'd forged, but standing up to him had helped to ease some of the anger she felt. The more she thought about it, the more she could understand the challenges he must have been going through. He seemed unable to remove his romantic feelings from their friendship, and while she struggled not to feel more, she felt the loss of the friendship the harshest. Yet considering the differences between their people, perhaps even a true friendship between them was too much to ask, let alone anything else. This journey had been a long one already and was not nearly over. While she wished that she hadn't lost the person that had become her closest friend along the way, she knew that first and foremost she had to continue to lead.

While she prepared the last of her things, she finally had one of the V'ahani women fix her hair. Rather than her typical braid, Latera was ready for a change. The woman ultimately cut her hair at her shoulders and tightly braided it into a crown. When it was finished, she felt brand new—at least until Elan abruptly approached her.

In stark contrast to his previously uncertain demeanor, Elan now stood tall and firm as he asked, "Latera, do you have a moment? I want to apologize and I would like to talk with you if you will let me. I have not been honest with you, or myself, but I would very much like to try and start." Without a word, she nodded her assent. "Great," he replied. "If we can go find a place to be alone, I will explain."

The two wandered off as Latera followed him away from the camp, wondering what he would say. Eventually, they came to a trail through a wooded area that took them out of sight. The trail led to a barren field that stood at the bottom of the same tall hill that she had scaled earlier. As Elan looked up to the top, she couldn't help but smirk. She nearly bumped into him as he abruptly stopped, turning to speak to her.

Just as he opened his mouth, however, he began squinting at something ahead. He pointed to it, "Do you see that?" he asked.

She did see something ahead, a figure of some kind. "Yes. What is it?"

They began walking a little further down the sloped plain toward it. When they got close enough, Latera noticed that it was a man with a pistol in his hand.

"Who is there and what are you doing out here?" Elan called to the man.

With a start the man turned around. It was Castor and he was now as pale as his clothing. "Oh!" he excitedly sighed. "Elan and Latera, hi. It is just me." Neither she nor Elan said anything. "I just came out for . . . you know . . . or maybe not." He looked up at the sky with a deep breath and continued, "There was a time when I used to live in the Mountainlands. When I did, there was a V'ahani man who was going through a very hard time and was depressed. One afternoon, while a group of us were hiking up in the hills we spotted him alone. Before we could reach him though he jumped over the ledge.

"The most unfortunate part of the story though was not that he jumped, but that he survived the fall. When we found him at the bottom, he could not move at all. We could see the life fading from him with each passing second, but almost as if to punish him it would not leave him entirely. Seeing his pain, we asked him if he wished for us to kill him out of mercy. We were dumbfounded when he declined. The reason he gave us though was that the instant he jumped from the ledge, he was overcome with regret. All his troubles had vanished in that moment as he realized how valuable his life was. So, as he lay there on the ground with his body broken, he told us that he felt fortunate to feel the pain that he was feeling."

Latera noticed a state of stillness descend over her. She felt nothing. No reaction was forthcoming, as if this moment was inevitable and she was only waiting for it to finish playing out before her.

"What does this story have to do with you?" Elan asked sharply.

Castor looked at Latera, and explained, "Only that when I did what I did, and I can see it in your eyes that you know what that was, I felt the same thing that man felt when he jumped. I felt immediate regret when I pulled that trigger, and now I stand here in the same condition emotionally that the man who jumped was in physically. I am utterly broken now. Unlike him though, my actions nullified the value of my life, rather than revealing it to me." With that, he looked down for a moment or two and began to weep. "There are pieces of things inside me that have splintered off. Love. Respect. Honor. Things that I used to defend and hold dear. I remember I used to look down at my shadow and see how tall it stood as a way to measure them. To measure myself . . . to tell myself how much of a man I had become. But now . . . now I cast no shadow, and all those pieces have faded away. Please, just grant me one thing," he cried. "I beg for nothing else but your forgiveness. Please."

Latera felt the urgent look Elan shot at her but ignored it. She refused to relinquish Castor's fear without his having earned it.

"Latera?" Elan pleaded.

With her stare, Castor continued to sob. It was as if she was communicating her betrayal to him without saying a word, and after all this time, he still didn't know what to say. "I am sorry," he whispered to her.

In that moment, she had accepted his fate as much as he had, and she felt a deep disappointment. She knew that his apology was hollow, and if he were truly sorry, then he'd help her save their people, as Arkouda would have wanted. Even now he had the opportunity to do so, but the coward simply couldn't. Then, he lifted his pistol to his head and pulled the trigger. Latera flinched for the slightest instant as her gaze followed his lifeless body to the ground.

Elan fell to his knees beside her. Breathing heavily, he uttered, "What just…"

Elan said nothing further, but even if he had, she was not sure she would have stopped in that moment to hear him. Latera had decided it was time to act. She lifted her hands to her mouth then and called up to the wind. Elan's eyes widened as the words came out. Soon after she had made her call, a group of vultures flew into view overhead. Latera was patient, allowing the group to circle their meal, below. Every minute of this ritual was intentional. She wanted Elan there to witness it, to see if he would protest, to see where his allegiance fell, but he said nothing. Finally, after giving him every opportunity to stop her, she gave a command and the scavengers descended upon Castor's body. Latera was once again still, watching without either pleasure or disgust as they tore away at the flesh of her father's killer. Elan, on the other hand, began heaving until he could hold it no longer and vomited on the ground below his feet.

Once Elan collected himself, Latera turned her attention toward him. "Tell me, Elan, what is it you wanted to talk about?"

As Elan proceeded to shamefully look away, she realized that no answer would come. With one last look at the gruesome scene before her, she marched toward the feasting vultures. There was no fear in her stride. Beside them, she spotted Castor's revolver, which she promptly lifted and tucked away. With that she turned to head back toward the camp, glancing up once again at the rocky hill she had climbed.

CHAPTER 9

POWDER

William and Judith got to know each other very intimately in the days following their wedding. In that time, they became inseparable, converging into one unit in both presence and thought. William was very pleased with their budding relationship. Visions filled his mind of the world that they would conquer together.

One afternoon, William, Judith, Blanton, Donna, and the Abigale family attended a local circus in Fayette. It was the first the Abigales had seen in the Murrieta and would surely be very different than what they were used to back home. The cities of the East were becoming much more industrialized, and demand for the talents of circus folk was in a significant decline. Many of the strangest characters were cast out for not conforming and traveled west to escape mistreatment. The Abigales cheered about each and every manner of deformity that surrounded them—from little people who appeared twice their age, to women with beards, to massive men who could lift obscene amounts of weight. The event that they chattered about the most, however, was the acrobatics.

As they approached the largest tent in the venue, Florence asked, "Mother, do you think one day I could learn to do the tricks that the acrobats do?"

"If you put enough effort into it, then there's nothing you can't do, my love," Maria replied.

Judith, whose hand was in William's as usual, added, "Yes, you could do those things, but you won't. You're an Abigale, and we're not people who join circuses."

"Don't talk to your sister that way, Judith," Maria implored as Florence kicked the dirt at her feet.

Out of the corner of William's eye, he saw Donna yank Blanton's shirt.

"My favorite so far was the strong man," the brother declared immediately. "I'd like to be as strong as him one day."

"The acrobats are my favorite part, too, Florence," Donna exhaled. "I hope they do the trick where they fly around on the bar!"

"Do you mean the trapeze?" Francis asked, looking not to Donna, but to Blanton for a response. Judith told William that Maria and she had spoken to the youngest Abigale about the situation with the twins the night before. During the talk he apparently mentioned thinking of them as a sort of circus act themselves, which William couldn't completely disagree with, though he promised not to give either a hard time anymore.

Blanton rolled his eyes and replied, "I think that's what she's talking about yes. I like the lion tamer, too."

"Yes, that's what I was talking about, the trapeze is the most amazing thing I've ever seen!" Donna responded as if Blanton had not even spoken.

William had always pitied the boy for that. Blanton was distressed at their arrangement and had once told Walter that at times he felt that his words were just noise that people ignored prior to hearing what Donna had to say.

They soon approached the massive, colorful main tent and took their seats among the crowd. As expected, the whole show was a spectacle the likes of which they hadn't seen before. Along with the trapeze and lion tamer, they beheld the thrills of the human cannonball, tightrope walker, and human pyramid. Each act that came out amazed more than the last, and overall it was very entertaining—even for the adults.

Just before the juggler was set to come out, William received a tap on the shoulder from behind. Paranoid at who would be interrupting him at such an event, he spun around. Judith turned as well. It was Gregory.

"Sir, there's something urgent that needs your attention back at the mansion."

"Well out with it, what could be so important?" he questioned.

"News from the North, sir," his right-hand-man replied. "News that you'll want to hear sooner rather than later."

William perked up knowing that this would be what he'd been waiting for. He turned to Judith, who nodded. The crowd was beginning to cheer for the jugglers, so in a loud voice William called to the others, "My dearest apologies everyone. There's been a key development that Judith and I must attend to. Please enjoy the rest of the show!"

Gregory led them back toward the mansion in record time. Standing on the front porch was a person whose face was almost completely bandaged. "William, hello!" the man suddenly called out. "It's a pleasure to meet you, sir!"

They shook hands once William arrived on the porch. "Hello there," William replied. "This is my wife Judith." Judith curtsied. "What's your name and what news do you bring me?"

"My name's Collin McCormack, and this is my assistant, Frankie Covington, sir," the man answered, pointing to the very young man who stood behind him and briefly waved. "I've come from Harran to tell you that Jeannie Morrell is alive. I saw her myself, but I did not have the resources I needed to capture her. A V'ahani boy and a skilled man are leading her north from Harran. Also, Jeannie isn't the only Morrell that remains alive. The eldest son, Harrison, is with them as well. Daniel sent me straight here to tell you what I witnessed."

William turned to Judith and, overwhelmed, gave her a huge kiss in his excitement. It felt as if there'd never been another way to react; it was so natural to him. She'd become his partner in this endeavor.

When he released her, she grinned broadly at him, and he cheered, "Please excuse me, but this is great news! Please, Collin, Frankie, come inside. We'll get your wounds taken care of by the best minds we have. And there's plenty to discuss."

*

A few hours had passed since the wolf attack, and Hanzah still remained unconscious. In an experience, which she admitted was nearly as traumatic as the attack itself, Jeannie had helped to wrap her friend's shattered arm back together. Much to her dismay, she could tell it wouldn't be very useful to him in its current state, and she worried about how he would take it when he woke. How she suffered from knowing she was the reason for it. It was her fault for pulling the trigger too soon. She had no idea how she could let herself slip like that. Once the messy deed of doctoring Hanzah's arm had been completed, she sat apart from the others and buried her face in her folded arms. She remained that way until she heard footsteps approach her.

"May I sit?" Harrison asked. Jeannie glanced behind him to make sure that Dominic was still with Hanzah before she nodded. Then her brother sat down by her side. "We're all terribly afraid, Jeannie," he admitted to her. "We're also each going to make mistakes, but we'll pick each other up from those mistakes."

"But what if those mistakes get us killed?" she retorted. "How will we just accept them as simple mistakes then, Harrison?"

"Jeannie, you ultimately saved Hanzah's life, not dashed it. It was you that left to go find him through the smoke. In that sense, you've already corrected your mistake and were very courageous when you did."

"I guess," she muttered.

"You should know it to be true," Harrison implored. "I assure you that even after what happened, that's how he'll see it, as well. If you hadn't killed that wolf, he wouldn't be here right now."

"But if I hadn't shot early, maybe the wolves would've never gotten to him at all." Even as she said it, she knew that what Harrison was saying was right. Perhaps she had managed to make up for her error in the end. "I just wish it were me in his place," she said with a sigh.

Harrison smiled. "It's understandable that you feel that way, too. You always were so caring, Jeannie. Mom and Dad would be so proud of you. Unfortunately, though, you can't take back what happened, so instead you'll need to do the next best thing and be his arm when he needs it."

"I will be," Jeannie promised. With Harrison's help, Jeannie's mind was more at ease, now. However, with the weather growing colder by the day, the first thing she thought of was the chill that ran down her spine. "Harrison, do you think we'll make it?" she asked. "Please, be honest."

"Of that I can't be certain," he admitted. "Only Hanzah knows how much further we have to go. Along with the weather, we're also running low on food, and our cover for shelter was partially damaged during the attack. So overall, I'd say the outlook isn't great if I was being honest."

Jeannie was silent, not knowing what to say as that sunk in.

"Then again," he continued, "I think we've come to learn that nothing is impossible, and I don't think our outlook has been particularly positive at all since we began this journey. So at least our current terribleness isn't as terrible as the potential for terrible that we could possibly experience on this long and terrible journey!"

She chuckled along with him for a moment. The normalcy of their familial bond was something they hadn't even had the opportunity to enjoy since being reunited.

"Well I suppose if we attempt to be terribly positive about this terrible situation, then it won't seem to be as terrible as it actually is," she played along with an ear-to-ear grin. "That might sound terrible, but would you disagree?"

"That doesn't sound terrible at all!" he quipped back. "What would be terrible is if we felt terribly terrible about the terribleness! So now Jeannie, I have to ask, do you still feel terrible?"

"Not terribly," she replied.

Harrison erupted in laughter, which was echoed by Jeannie. Just a moment with her brother and she felt more positive than she had in days. The Kennedales would never know how grateful she was to them.

A few minutes later, Dominic approached them. "Hanzah is awake," he said. Jeannie turned to Harrison excitedly, now confident in her ability to help her friend through this.

*

Not long after the gunshot was fired from beyond the hills, Lennox and Parish came rushing to the scene, where the vultures were picking apart Castor's body. When they crossed the rocky hill, they immediately lifted their arms over their noses and turned back from the grisly sight. As for Latera, she had hardly noticed the insignificant councilmen had arrived.

"What happened here?" Lennox asked her, slowing his horse as he approached her. Rather than replying, she continued walking right past them without a word. There was an icy rage inside her that was colder than the winter air. She would be sure that they felt its bite.

She heard Elan's voice then. He must have been following a few paces behind her. "We were heading out there to talk, and he thought he was there alone. It seemed he was trying to come to terms with what he had done, but in the end it was too much, so he took his own life."

"What do you mean that he had 'come to terms with what he had done'? What had he done?" Parish grunted.

"She knows. I know, too," Elan replied angrily. "I have not told and will not tell anyone. I do not care about your quarrels as long as we reach the Hold safely."

The councilmen stared at Elan, before flicking nervous glances her way. She ignored them, her cold stillness having descended in their presence as it had in Castor's. She was done pretending.

Lennox finally replied, "We know your intentions are true, Elan. For the sake of both our peoples, you must maintain this secret and convince Latera to do the same. We alone allowed this allegiance to happen when it needed to happen and for it to come to fruition smoothly our people must know only that and nothing else."

A look of disgust covered Elan's face for a moment, before it smoothed over. "Of course, I will not tell them. We are too close to our destination for a rebellion." He cast a glance at her, a question on his brow. She did not answer it. "But I have no control over Latera. No one does. I do not believe anyone ever did."

A small thrill sang through her then. Elan had recognized the fire growing inside her, even if the councilmen were blind to it. They may no longer be friends; they may no longer care for one another—but for better or worse, they were allies, and she had his respect. And that was all she needed to lead her people alongside his when the time came.

When she said nothing, Elan continued, "Latera has known for some time though and said nothing. She well knows that we are too close to liberating both of our clans to risk division now. For that, I believe she will not tell them—at least, not yet."

She watched as Lennox and Parish exchanged a gloomy look, and it nourished her.

"We appreciate your understanding, Elan," Parish exhaled, ignoring her presence entirely. "Now tell us more about what happened here. We just want to be sure we have the whole story."

She gave the slightest of nods to Elan, and turned back toward the camp, uncaring to hear more. In her heart was a force that she could no longer hold down. It was a fuse that had been lit with the revelation of her father's murder and detonated with Castor's plea for a forgiveness he had not earned. She felt not a trace of fear, doubt, or remorse for those that would dare to stand in her way.

When she reached the grounds, she called out, "V'ahani! Gather around me!"

The weary and curious clansmen emerged from their cover and fixed their eyes upon the daughter of their former Chieftain. Before them all, she was not just becoming a woman, but becoming a leader.

"Along this way, you have been made to believe something that is untrue," she declared. "You have been made to believe that you cannot complete this journey from the Riverlands of the North to the Tokali Hold of the South. The ones who have stalked us have tried to convince us that they are more powerful than we are and that we are at their mercy. I am here now, the daughter of the great Arkouda, to tell you that this cannot be further from the truth. There will be no breaking of the V'ahani. We will not be starved; we will not be intimidated; we will survive!"

Cheers rang out from the men and women around her. They

energized her in a way she'd never experienced before.

"The Keagans know that if we reach the Hold, we will be strengthened," she rallied. "They are the ones who should be afraid! No matter what happens before we make it there, we must remain strong. They will try to hunt us down like animals, so let us show them that the V'ahani cannot be tamed. This gang will rue the day they stepped foot into OUR lands. My friends, my brothers, my sisters, my family, that is exactly what the ground you stand on is. These are our plains, our fields. The Riverlands are ours, and the North is OURS! With our Tokali brothers, the South is now ours, too! No gang can take this Territory away from us! We will not let them. We will fight!"

She lifted her fist into the air as every single one of her people followed suit. Men, women, and children all wailed at the top of their lungs in unison. Though happiness in the truest sense of the word was not something Latera could currently feel, she grinned at her peoples' enthusiasm. As Lennox, Parish, and Elan returned, she saw the look of confusion on their faces. They had no idea what had caused the sudden rush of excitement. Latera noted this with pleasure before she disappeared into her tent.

*

At first, everything was very fuzzy for Hanzah. He looked up and could see three people sitting before him. Once his focus returned to him, he could see it was his parents and sister. He sat across from them in a room with his arms folded on a table.

"Where am I?" he asked in a daze.

"You are home," his mother replied warmly.

He shook his head in confusion. "But, Mama, Father, how can this be?"

"Because you are always home, son," his father, Arkouda, replied, "and we will always be with you."

Hanzah looked up at his father and finally began to rejoice that his family was around him. With a glimmer of hope, he nervously asked, "So . . . was it all just a dream?"

His family all laughed together and looked back at him. He wondered why they ignored his question, but things suddenly began changing. The room was once again becoming blurry, and his family was slowly fading before his eyes. In desperation he reached out toward them, however, his forearm was also beginning to disappear. In the madness, he was overcome with a sharp pain, and just as his horror reached its peak, he opened his eyes with a gasp.

He was back in the cold. The three people that he could now make out were Dominic, who was sitting beside him, and Jeannie and Harrison sitting apart a little distance away. The pain, the likes of which he had never felt, remained. The panic from his dream did not end, either, as he looked down at his broken forearm. For a moment, he lost sight of what was the nightmare and what was reality.

"Don't be afraid, Hanzah," Dominic assured him. "You're going to be all right. Just give me a moment to get the others."

Hanzah grew emotional as he recognized the futility of his situation. How would he make it through the perils they would surely face without the use of his arm? When the others approached him, he did find some small relief that he could actually touch the people who were in his presence this time.

"What happened?" he asked, only partially wanting to hear the answer.

"The wolves," Dominic started, "one of them got ahold of you. I'm sorry, my friend. I tried my best to distract them and fend them off. Do you not remember?"

"It is hazy, but I remember parts," he replied.

"Dominic shouldn't be apologizing," Jeannie jumped in. "It was my fault the last wolf was able to get to us. I was afraid and fired the shot before I should have."

This confused Hanzah. "Actually, one of the only things I clearly remember is you saving my life, Jeannie," he recounted. "I thought I was finished when you appeared out of the smoke and downed the wolf that had me in its jaws."

Jeannie smiled with Harrison. "Well if you need anything at all, please just ask," she pleaded. "We're family now and we're here to get you through this."

"Speaking of getting through this," Harrison changed the subject, "I know you're just waking from an awful experience, and I can't imagine what must be going through your head, but what happened has delayed us quite a bit. With our supplies dwindling and conditions in these mountains worsening, we must continue on as soon as possible, or I fear we won't make it the rest of the way. I'm not sure how organized your thoughts are at the moment, but do you know about how much further we should have to go to your uncle's camp?"

Hanzah pondered the remaining distance. "I would say we're about another day away now," he explained. "We might have been able to make it by this evening originally, but with the wolves having set us back, I think we might be able to arrive by tomorrow morning or afternoon."

"Well then if you're up to continue, we should get moving now," Harrison said. "The clouds are growing dark this afternoon, and we can't afford to extend this trip any longer than it already has been."

"Like Jeannie said," Dominic added, "we're at your service completely, Hanzah. Whatever it is that you need assistance with, we'll give it."

Hanzah felt gratitude for a moment, to have made such true friends so quickly after he believed himself alone in the world. "I am ready to continue."

As Harrison had mentioned, the sky was quickly darkening. For the remainder of the day, they trekked the sloped path in horrific storm conditions. Through snow, dirt, and intense winds, Hanzah pushed on, exerting himself as much as his body could handle. He thought of his uncle Orrin and other relatives who would welcome him when he arrived. If nothing else, he felt that just being near family again would bring him peace. It was his main motivation now to fight through his exhaustion.

By the time the evening came, his face was icy and frostbitten. They had made great progress through the day, and he indicated to the others that they were drawing closer. The storm however was also at its most intense at this time with thunder and lightning raging through the clouds. The enormous sound of each flash echoed through the entire mountain range as if they were captured in a glass. Hanzah's ears rang as the comrades were forced to shout for communication.

"Should we rest?" Harrison yelled out. "It doesn't seem safe for us to be out in this weather for too long."

"I think that's a good idea!" Dominic called back. "Let's set up ov—"

Suddenly the loudest strike of the evening blared overhead. The sky lit up blue as a massive bolt impacted the mountain beside them. When it hit the cliff, a plume of snow burst into the air. Hanzah's heart sank as he saw that more snow was now rapidly flowing downward in their direction.

"Avalanche! Run!" he howled at the top of his lungs. The others didn't hesitate to follow his command. They ran as fast as their legs could carry them. At some point however, there would be no outrunning the rushing snow.

"We must stay together!" Dominic cried, making the connection that the snow was bound to hit them. "If we're separated there will be no hope!" As quickly as they could, they all joined hands and were almost simultaneously overcome by the flowing snow. In the wave that carried them, they were dragged like pieces of debris.

Hanzah held onto Dominic's hand for as long as he could, but with his stronger arm broken, the force was too great to maintain his grip for long. He soon became separated from the others and felt his consciousness fading.

Sometime later, he came around. The avalanche had ended. His surroundings had changed from mayhem to tranquility, but he could hardly move a muscle due to his pain, exhaustion, hunger, and thirst. Around him there was no sight of Jeannie, Harrison, or Dominic. Then he turned his head upward, looking straight at the clear sky, and hope began to leave him. He could feel himself slowly fading away with it. As his sight blurred, his focus shifted to movement in the tree closest to him. On a branch had landed a single, tiny swallow. The bird looked at the boy with its head tilted crookedly. It brought a smile to his face. It made him feel as if he wasn't alone as he lay there. Using whatever breath remained in him, he began mumbling to it and continued doing so until the moment his exhaustion overtook him.

*

For some days more, the V'ahani traveled through various terrains toward the Hold. They survived on whatever tiny animals and plants they could find, but in this region, especially at this time of year, food was few and far between. As much as Latera tried to keep morale up vocally, the only thing that seemed to keep them going at this point was Elan's acknowledgement one morning that they were only a day's travel away from their destination. There had been no further contact between them, but she didn't feel it was needed then. Maybe once they made it to the Hold, they could talk more. They would need to if they were to smoothly guide their tribes into a stable alliance. Perhaps one day, in time, they could be more than allies again. For now, she would just be glad once her people were safe and fed.

By midday, the lack of food distracted the V'ahani from their progress. It was just becoming unbearable—even to Latera—when once again a camp appeared in the distance.

"The Tokali have come through for us again!" Lennox shouted as the V'ahani rejoiced.

Like the last camp, from the distance they could see no inhabitants. However, there was what appeared to be a small fire burning in the middle. They stampeded toward it. Closer and closer, they came until they were within no more than a couple hundred feet of the camp. Suddenly, a single, massive explosion filled the sky. Those who were closest were blown back off their horses. The others were terrified and scurried back in retreat. When they reached a position of perceived safety, Parish called for them to stand their ground. Before them, there was a massive plume of smoke and flames engulfing the now flattened grounds. Latera wondered in despair how this could have happened. Their only hope of sustenance had just vanished before them.

Lennox rushed to Elan and shoved him to the ground. "What have you led us to, Tokali?!"

"This was not my people, I swear it!" Elan pleaded. "This was the Keagans, it had to be!"

Latera thought that Elan must be right, but wondered how she could trust anyone's word at this point. She watched silently as Parish approached Elan and pressed a rifle against his forehead. "Tell us again that you knew nothing about this," Parish demanded. Some of the V'ahani begged him to stop, while others said nothing. It was telling of her people's current trust in the Tokali.

Elan finally locked eyes with Latera. For the first time in days, other than when addressing her people, her stone cold stillness cracked, a sliver of apprehension sliding through. She could see it in him that this trick wasn't Elan's doing.

He stared at her and begged, "I knew noth—" His plea stopped abruptly as his eyes shifted, focusing into the distance toward the billowing smoke that was behind her. "Look there! A man!" Elan shouted, and sure enough, when Latera turned, someone could be seen running away from the flattened village.

"After him!" Lennox screamed.

They chased at full speed. Latera's horse moved so fast that it felt as if she'd left the ground entirely to fly. Within minutes they were upon him, but it was Lennox who knocked the man to the ground. Infuriated, he began to beat the man, who wore a lion's paw pin.

A Keagan, then, she thought furiously.

Without Parish's eventual restraint, Lennox would have likely not stopped until the man was dead.

"How did you do this?!" Lennox exclaimed. "Where are the rest of your men?!"

The culprit's face and mouth were filled with blood. Now lying on his back he rolled back and forth, laughing maniacally. "We're everywhere!" the man chirped.

Parish once again lifted his rifle. "That was not an answer to his question," he declared. "You have one more opportunity to explain."

The man didn't flinch with a rifle in his face and continued laughing. "You know, back east there aren't any real gods. Did you know that?"

"What are y—" Lennox started.

"Back east there are no real gods, and even if there were, there'd be no messiahs honest enough to reveal them. But here . . ." he hummed as he lifted his outstretched arms into the air. "Here in the Murrieta the gods walk among us. Here, they reveal themselves!"

"Is this really what you want?" Lennox asked, motioning to Parish's rifle.

"I should ask you the same question," he replied. His eyes then turned to Elan, who he winked at before cackling loudly behind more bloody coughs.

Without delay, Elan drew his gun on the man and said, "Is something funny about me?"

Latera had seen enough. Before the Keagan Gang member could answer, she swung down from her horse, and in full view of the gathered V'ahani, came with Castor's pistol in her hand. She stood over the maniac, blocking out the light from above him. "Wherever it is that you think you are about to go, I promise you that your gods will not save you when you arrive," she uttered coldly.

"He already h—"

The bullet plunged into his skull, silencing him. The Keagan man didn't get to finish his last words, because Latera didn't feel he deserved them.

All the others stood quietly, watching her. "We must go now," she declared. "There is no telling how far behind they are, so we must hurry. Despite what he says, we will achieve our goal. We will reach the Hold."

They did not cheer this time as Latera marched away through the crowd, but they did continue to follow her all the same.

CHAPTER 10

FOR THE WORLD TO SEE

With the smoke from the demolished camp at their backs, the V'ahani made their final push toward the Hold. Their horses raced onward as if the Keagans were right behind them. For all they knew, the gang very well could have been after what had just occurred. Hunger and fear combined into an overwhelming sense of desperation. From the moment she had pulled the trigger on the attacker, Latera continued to lead the way, with Elan only shouting out occasional orders for direction. In sight and in mind, she was the clear symbol that kept the V'ahani from abject surrender. Lennox and Parish simply became part of the group. Not only was their confidence waning, but also even their desire to lead had all but vanished. They were not equipped mentally or emotionally to guide the V'ahani like Latera was. She had known this for a time now and accepted their realization of it with no fanfare.

Dust clouds filled the air at their heels. Along the way, Latera saw multiple heads turning back to ensure that they were not being trailed. But Latera did not look back—only forward. With their spirit nearly broken, Latera knew that capture by the Keagans would surely be the final straw for her people. She would need to be the symbol that demanded them to fight on. So she became it.

For hours they rode with their vision progressively fading and with breaths turning to gasps.

Then, after a period of riding through a densely wooded area, Elan made the call. "We are approaching!"

"We are almost there my brothers and sisters!" Latera declared.

Sure enough, a few minutes later, they cleared the trees that surrounded them and the gates of the Hold came into view. Cheers filled the mass of the convoy. It seemed as if even the horses knew what the city would mean for them, and they whinnied along with the cheers. Confidence swept over Latera as she looked out on the massive Hold. It reminded her in some ways of the Great Fortress. She envisioned the streets inside being lined with Tokali the same way the Fortress was with V'ahani in the North. The height of its walls was intimidating in that they showed the danger of what they were built to keep out. However, she rejoiced in the fact that at least a place this vast would not likely explode before her peoples' eyes.

Elan guided his horse to the front. "I will lead the way to the gates," he explained to Latera. "Follow me slowly. Once the guards see me, everything will be all right. We will get you all inside and fed."

Latera looked at him for a moment before nodding her assent. "Very well. Lead the way."

She then turned back to the V'ahani to explain the need for calm and caution. As hard as it must have been for them to be patient in their final trot to their destination, Elan's promise of food and rest was too appealing for her people not to follow his instructions. As their horses began to walk through the final stretch of field, which was approximately 500 yards, they noticed movement in the guard towers. Gasps could be heard amongst them when they recognized that several men were beginning to take aim.

"Elan, why are they pointing weapons at us?" Latera calmly asked.

"This is standard," Elan quietly replied, "You can never be too sure of who will come knocking in these parts."

This was not a response that would help the others remain calm, however, so she did not share it. She simply projected confidence and calm as her people looked to her. Meanwhile, her mind churned in circles. Without familiarity with this southern sector of the Murrieta, the possibilities of threats were limitless. The grizzlies did not roam these parts, so they would not be there to provide protection. Their only line of defense was the few rifles and petty weapons that they carried, which essentially meant that they were defenseless. When they reached the middle of the wide-open field, their vulnerability to attack from each and every angle was evident and unsettling. With each breeze that passed by, Latera's body felt every chill. The wooded area that they had emerged from was noisy in the gusting wind, and the suggestive sounds it emitted made her cringe. There were already weapons pointed at their front, but Latera held an even greater fear of what could come from behind. Every bit of clacking from the steps of the horses rang in her ears like the beating of a drum. She looked in the sky, desperate to call up to the wind for a sweeping of the area. However, she did not want to alert the guards or worry her people any more than they already were, so she remained silent.

"STOP THERE!" one of the tower guards suddenly yelled out. The bravado of his voice was alarming, but with a deep breath,

Latera began to feel better about how close they now were to entering the Hold. "What is your business here?" the same guard followed.

Elan approached the front of the crowd and looked up at the guards. "It is me, Elan, son of Malik and Adila, and I have come with our allies, the V'ahani of the Riverlands."

When they saw him, they turned to one another and nodded. One of the guards remained with his gun now at ease, while the other retreated out of sight from his post.

The remaining guard then replied, "Hold, Elan," before falling silent.

The tension did not ease in Latera. The moments stretched painfully on, until finally, the gates began to slowly open. A sigh of relief was emitted in unison from the tired, weary V'ahani. After all they had been through, they were here at long last. They could finally re-supply and replenish their malnourished bodies. There would now be a fighting chance for them against the ever-growing power of the Keagans. As the doors opened, there was more movement by the guard towers. The second guard, who smiled and waved at Elan, returned with a man and woman who did the same. He smiled back at them until they rushed back down out of the tower to greet him and the others at the gates.

Once the gates had opened, Latera motioned to her people and the V'ahani slowly approached the Hold. When they entered, there was no one in sight except the man, the woman and the guards.

"Greetings, friends!" the man exclaimed warmly. "We are so pleased that you were able to make it here safely! We tried our very best to facilitate your safe passage along the way but thankfully that is all behind you now. My name is Malik, and this is my wife Adila, we are the parents of your guide, Elan."

"We cannot thank you enough for your graciousness," Lennox declared, stepping forward and dusting off his leadership again. Latera allowed him to do so; she wanted to observe their new surroundings before she announced herself in any way. She also was aware that though she'd become the symbol for her people, she had yet to formally become their leader, and now was not the time to challenge for that role.

Lennox took a breath and continued, "We would not have made it here alive otherwise. However, we ran into some additional trouble at the second camp we found, so if you might have some food to spare for us, our people need it. I believe they have earned it. I am Lennox, by the way, the Chieftain of the V'ahani of the Riverlands."

A concerned look crossed Adila's face. "Of course, we have plenty—a feast—to go around for everyone," she replied. "Whatever you all need, we have. But please tell me, what kind of trouble did you come across at our camp?"

This time Latera spoke for them and explained, "A Keagan man rigged the camp before we reached it. As we approached, he leveled every last bit of it in a great explosion."

Malik and Adila turned to look at each other. "This is very troubling," Malik said, pausing before adding, "Of course, this is also why you are here. Only together can we unify the Murrieta. We will worry about that once you are back to your full strength though."

"Yes, please join the rest of our people in the Square!" Adila chimed. "We have prepared a feast and celebration to welcome you and signify our unification. As your leader says, you all deserve it!"

"Oh and hopefully our Elan was a good host on the journey here! We are very proud of the sacrifice he has made," Malik cheered, before turning to Elan. "Son, if you could please come with us while the V'ahani are led to the Square, we would like to welcome you back ourselves." Elan nodded and walked off with his parents with his head hung down.

Was he upset that she did not sing his praises to his father? She shrugged off the idea, and focused on her people. The mouths of the V'ahani watered as they followed the guards toward the Square. They were excited to meet their allies and begin their work together, but at that time they were much more focused on regaining their strength. Latera could hear snippets of conversation all around her to that effect. It reminded her of her desire to send a bird to Hanzah, if only she knew where to send it. All she hoped for was to receive word from him soon that he had safely reached the Mountainlands camp, so she could in turn let her brother know she'd made it to the Hold, and kept their people safe along the way.

Trekking through the streets of the Hold was almost as agonizing as pacing through the field to the gates. Each corner they turned and each set of homes they weaved through came up short of the mountain of food and celebration that they had envisioned. When the guards finally stopped in an open area that they could immediately tell was the Square, their anticipation had reached its highest point.

Observing the area, Latera saw they were surrounded by some of the larger buildings the Hold had to offer, with balconies on each side of the Square. She couldn't help but admire the beauty and composition of it. A great fire had been lit in the center of the Square, as if to emphasize the architecture surrounding it. The greatest of all, though, was the largest of the balconies at the head of the Square, which seemed to look over everything. The top of the balcony reminded her of the hill she had climbed. She envisioned the feeling she would get addressing her people from such a perch. What it would be like to be above it all—this was a new thought that was now ever prevalent in her mind.

After minutes of standing there in wait, she noticed the guards begin to back away from the group slowly. Then she had a sharp realization. From the moment they entered the Hold, all the way along their march to the Square, there was still no one around. She wondered where they could all be hiding—and why.

"We will be right back to fetch everyone!" One of the guards suddenly cheered. "Just a moment please!"

Then Latera's stomach dropped as the final heartbreaking oddity registered in her—not a single one of the Tokali she had seen at this point in the Hold, not the guards or Elan's parents, was wearing orange. That could only mean one thing: it was too late.

As she looked up in horror, there emerged a swarm of men and women with weapons drawn from the balconies. Every single one of those who appeared wore brown clothing, and on the chests that were within her sight, she could see the Keagan pins. It was what was behind the apparel however, that was most devastating to Latera. These men and women were not just Easterners in the ranks of the Keagans. Within the crowd of militants were Tokali, as well.

Elan's "mission" became clear to her then. The V'ahani of the Riverlands had been herded like sheep southward, out of their home and into a place already controlled by the very gang they had sought to help defend it from. She didn't know why they would do this, but understood the gravity of the mistake her people had made. She was glad that Hanzah was not here with her in that moment. He was still free.

The truth behind Elan's behavior had finally become clear to her as well. The reason why they could not be friends—let alone something more. This was a crime that she would never forgive him for, not as long as she breathed.

The surrounded V'ahani were thrown into a state beyond terror. By now, they were well past that. Latera knew they were simply broken. She could see it in each of them. They no longer had the energy to fear, to fight, or to run. They accepted that whatever fate the Keagans had planned for them would be the only peace they would now find.

This became even more evident when Latera recognized Walter Keagan, Elan, and Elan's parents among those emerging from the main balcony. Along with them were two other Keagan men as well. One of them took the lead, looking upon the Square with a sinister grin.

"Welcome to the south y'all!" he shrieked. "How was the trip down here? Was it comfortable? How about the sights and sounds?"

Some of the other Easterners began to giggle at the dejected V'ahani.

While Latera's fiery gaze was fixed on a clearly ashamed Elan, her people looked straight down at the ground. They did not dare to say a word or move a muscle as the Keagan man continued.

"Not a talkative bunch quite yet, huh?" he resumed. "Well, my name is Clovis Keagan. I'm a brother of William Keagan. This here is my associate Devin Turpin, and I take it y'all have already become acquainted with everyone else up here, so I won't give any unnecessary introductions.

"But hear this, I know most of y'all are afraid, and, if so, then that's a good thing. Y'all should be afraid. In fact, y'all should be downright fucking terrified, because if there's even a consideration being given to disobeying us Keagans, then there is only one thing that will happen. I don't need to tell y'all what that is, but I want to because I'm enjoying this look on y'all's pitiful faces, so shit, I'll tell you right now that you will die. It won't be a pleasant death neither, my friends. To avoid this outcome, y'all will trade with who we tell you to trade with, fight for us when we tell you to fight, and recognize that you are no longer Va-Ha-Ni or whatever the fuck it is you were before. Y'all are Keagans now. If I'm not mistaken, unification was the reason you tribesmen followed this bold young man Elan down here anyway, wasn't it? He showed us how far the Tokali were willing to go to prove their loyalty. Now it's y'all's turn to join the fun. We have united y'all with the Tokali AND the East, so it seems to me like y'all got your wish in the end—thanks to us. You're welcome."

Clovis Keagan had the most sinister smile Latera had ever seen. Like a hungry, rabid wolf, he looked down on them, and she felt, even in her anger, a trickle of fear enter her.

"Now let me tell you one more thing, no one needs to get hurt, so please, make some sort of noise or something if y'all agree to these terms of which you have no real say in!" Still none made a sound, but they now turned their somber, starving faces toward the balcony. "Well I kind of figured I wouldn't get much of a reply," Clovis called. "But I have a feeling that'll all change in a moment. See, I KNOW that some of y'all are familiar with my cousin Walter, so maybe he'll be able to get through this wall of shyness there seems to be. Walter, you did have something to say now didn't you? Please, step forward!"

Walter Keagan stumbled forward with the help of his cane and appeared very pleased to be standing over his previous captors. "I do certainly have something to say," Walter exclaimed. "I believe we all got off on the wrong foot when I first met you folks, and I'd like to right that wrong today so that we can move forward together. If y'all could first please forgive my cousin. He did lie about one thing, and that was the fact that none of y'all would be hurt today." Gasps could be heard from the crowd. Some began to cry and beg for mercy. "Oh no," he continued, "Don't get me wrong. The innocent will be spared of that y'all can be sure. But there are snakes in y'all's midst. Would your noblest of councilmen please step forward?"

Lennox and Parish remained in place with their heads down.

After a second or two of waiting, Clovis took charge in outrage. "I know we waited some time for your arrival, but we're not otherwise a patient bunch!" he cried. "If you bastards don't step forward, or if the rest of you do not cast these councilmen out, then you should all prepare for a storm of bullets!"

The V'ahani hurriedly located and pushed the councilmen forward. Lennox and Parish fell to their knees for all to see. Latera noted the utter defeat in them. In a way, somewhere deep inside, she was almost thankful just for that. It was the only justice she would see, for their deaths at the hands of the Keagans would not qualify as just. No death at the hand of a Keagan could.

"Thank you!" Walter cheered. "How are you, boys?" he snickered joyfully. "It's been some time since I last saw y'all. The days don't seem to have been kind either. Let me ask, did y'all tell these folks yet how this whole thing began? I'm sure y'all did, right?" He waited for a moment and they did not move. Parish actually began to cry.

"No?" Walter mocked. "Well then, let me be the story teller. You see, these two brave souls captured me back at the river when I was in the middle of some important business. The thing about it was that they had other intentions in mind than just my capture. Yes sir, there's a darkness in them that even us Keagans can't stomach. After they managed to best me, these traitorous vermin went and killed y'all's Chieftain."

The V'ahani began to erupt in shock and outrage, but Latera saw what Walter Keagan was doing. He was giving them a villain beside himself.

Walter continued over them. "Now, I didn't much care for the man, but I saw that he was at least honorable and did not deserve to be fallen by his own council! I guess they didn't see what I saw, though, because they each sent a bullet right through him and shot him dead into the river. He bled so much, he turned that River White of yours crimson, I swear. Isn't that right, you greedy bastards?"

Jeers turned into screams, and the guards were soon forced to control the riotous crowd.

"Bring them to the balcony!" Clovis ordered, feeding off the furor in the Square.

As they were escorted, two ropes were thrown over the terrace. The cheers only intensified at the sight. Latera could see that somehow the Keagans were actually winning her people over. She struggled to think of something she could do to change that, to remind them of the Keagan villainy, to remind them of their true enemy. She had to act now. If she were to lose her people emotionally to these men, she knew there would be no hope to overcome their enslavement.

When the two men reached the top, the crowd began to settle down in anticipation. Latera knew this would be her chance to be heard. "Coward!" she screamed up at Elan, as ropes were prepared for the men. He looked at her with wide eyes, attempting to silently urge her to stop. Cared for her safety, did he? The danger was all his doing.

"How could you do this to us?" she yelled. "This whole time you were just leading us to this? We were led to believe that the Tokali were a proud clan, yet you are anything but! You are all weak! You are all scum!"

Clovis let out an impressed chuckle that was echoed by Walter and Devin. "Well I see y'all have a brave one amongst you!" He said. "Unfortunately, we can't have that. Bring her up next, and anyone else who has a problem!"

The V'ahani began to protest furiously as the guards apprehended Latera. Their reaction was all that she'd hoped it would be. Their cries surrounded her until she was thrown to her knees on the balcony and could hear Elan protesting. His vehemence surprised her; he fought harder even than her people.

"NO!" he implored. "She is the one I told you about! You promised that no harm would come of her!"

Except the harm he caused her and her people, Latera thought.

"Elan, stop this, please," his father pleaded.

Clovis looked at the boy and then at his parents.

"Is there going to be a problem?" Devin asked them.

"No, of course not!" Adila assured them, to which Elan fell silent.

An echo of Latera's earlier thought came to her. His true feelings did not matter if this was where his final decision fell. He was nothing but a traitor. He was never a friend.

Clovis' amusement remained in his voice as he turned back to the Square. "Are you ready to watch these traitors hang, my people?!" he asked the crowd. The cheers from the V'ahani were now less enthusiastic, but the volume was even greater now as the surrounding Easterners began showing their excitement as well. "Walter, would you like to take one, and I'll take the other?"

"With pleasure," Walter replied. The nooses were placed around the two men's necks and they were forced to the end of the balcony with guns to their heads.

"Climb up on the ledge," Clovis demanded. Only Parish, who was Walter's to push, followed the order.

"I will not," Lennox cried with his body shaking.

"I'm afraid it wasn't a fucking request, you dimwit," Clovis laughed as he pressed his pistol harder against the Chieftain's temple. "Get up there now or get shot."

Lennox peered nervously down at the ground below. "I would rather be shot then."

Clovis shrugged. "Fair enough," he muttered. He then loosened the noose and released it from Lennox's neck. Lennox's face was briefly filled with relief when suddenly Clovis lunged full force and tackled him over the ledge. Latera leapt up from her knees and no one stopped her. Their gazes were all riveted on the pair as they fell more than twenty feet toward the ground with Clovis tightly grappling his victim. The man was truly mad. The Square was silent in anticipation. After what felt like an eternity, they hit the ground. Actually, only Lennox hit the ground, with Clovis using his body to break the fall. Though he was bloodied and bruised from the impact, the Easterners cheered for their leader. An initially shocked Walter shook his head and soon after pushed Parish to hang.

The fall and impact of Clovis' body was somehow not enough to kill Lennox, who after reaching the ground lay writhing in pain. His attacker rolled around cackling in his own merry agony next to him. "You said you would shoot!" Lennox screamed. "Why?!"

Clovis looked up at the V'ahani. "I did, didn't I!?" he shrieked at them. "Well I don't keep oaths for those that don't keep oaths!" The Square responded noisily. "The fun doesn't end!" Clovis rallied. "It just doesn't ever end!" Then he climbed on top of Lennox and began mercilessly beating the man's face in with his gun and fists and anything he could swing. Parish continued to dangle as this occurred and the crowd was sent into a frenzy. Blow after blow, brought Lennox closer to death. Latera was most deeply disturbed not by the violence itself, but by Clovis' enjoyment of it.

After some time of carrying on, just before his knuckles popped out of his skin, Clovis was finished. He stood up victoriously and screamed at the top of his lungs, first in the face of his victim and then toward his audience. After some cheering however, the crowd went quiet as croaking could be heard from Lennox. Latera actually now pitied him as she wondered how he could possibly still be alive.

"Let him bleed!" Clovis called as he began walking back toward the stairs to the main balcony.

Then, just as Parish ceased struggling and let out his last gasping breath, a shot rang out from the Square that silenced Lennox once and for all.

After realizing what had happened, Malik looked out in horror and yelled, "Gannon, no!"

Looking back, Clovis started to laugh. "Well, I guess he got the bullet he asked for after all!" he shouted, as he almost simultaneously became furious. "Whoever that was, take that little shit away immediately! I'll deal with him later."

There was a pause while the young man named Gannon was apprehended, and the others in the Square got a grip on all that had just occurred. Latera thought she'd like to meet this Gannon, the only Tokali she'd seen to show honor and courage. She thought they might get along. It was a wistful thought, as wistful as getting a chance to say goodbye to Hanzah, considering that she was about to die.

Once Clovis reached the top of the balcony, he interrupted the silence. "So who's next?" he squealed.

Latera was then brought forward and the begging in the crowd for mercy commenced.

"STOP!" Elan demanded as the rope was eventually placed around her neck.

"Would your boy like to join her?" Clovis snarled at Malik.

"Do you hear the anguish of the people below?" Elan pleaded. "She is clearly important to them. I have seen it. She is more of a leader to them than either of the men you just killed. You want them on our side, do you not? Do you remember the Chieftain that Walter mentioned was killed? This is his daughter! They will go as she goes!"

Latera looked at Elan a moment. How hard he tried to save her touched some part of her. It wasn't enough to forgive him, but it was something. Perhaps their friendship had not been a complete lie. Yet, in this moment, he failed to understand that she'd die for the sake of her people, and she'd do it gladly. She'd do anything for them, anything so that their spirit may live to fight again another day. It hit her then that they had that in common in the end. He'd do anything for his people, including destroy her own. If the Tokali truly had no choice but to submit to the Keagans, then maybe he had just done what he needed to do as well. After all, this is what a leader did: put the people first.

"They will go as she goes!" Elan repeated desperately.

Clovis grew angrier, though Latera hadn't thought that possible. He looked to Walter and Devin.

"Killing her is something that William and Daniel would probably like for me to refrain from doing, would you agree?" he asked.

Devin nodded. "It would most certainly seem that way to me, yes," he submitted. "They probably wouldn't have wanted the councilmen to be killed either, but that actually worked in our favor with these people. Killing this girl might not have the same impact, I imagine."

"Very well," Clovis exhaled.

Latera had barely absorbed the fact that the maniac that was Clovis Keagan could see reason—let alone that she would not be a martyr this day—when he shot her a dark, hungry look. Clovis slowly moved his hands to her neck, and turning his gaze back to Elan, he worked the rope in his hands, but, rather than untying it, he actually tightened its grip on her throat to see Elan's reaction. Latera could not see what he saw, but Clovis's gleeful smile told her that he had managed to find a new weakness to exploit in Elan—her.

Then he turned his dead, crazed eyes back on her. "You know what will happen if your people try to revolt against us, don't you?" he whispered to Latera.

"Yes," she said, as sternly as she could. She would not cower in front of this man, not in front of her people. She knew he brought death, but if she survived this moment, she would make sure that he lived to regret it. Her people may be broken, but she could piece them back together. Yet, the feel of his fingers on her skin was cold and hardly felt human, so against her will, she began to shake— or perhaps the reaction was because of the fact that she could no longer breathe. Just as black spots began to dance in her vision, he expertly untied the rope and let her free.

"Now please, my new comrades, eat!" Clovis cheered upon turning to the V'ahani in the Square. He then stormed off with Walter and Devin as her starving people rejoiced. The giddiness that pervaded in his display seemed to vanish as his men and he departed.

With Elan and his parents' attention fixed on her, Latera walked out to the balcony to behold her people. She once again didn't know whether to be pleased or terrified by their excitement and relief, but there was one thing that sat inside her like a pit in her stomach, one fact that broke her heart right then and there. Regardless of what came tomorrow, as the V'ahani now celebrated that they may finally eat and rest, Latera realized that the Riverlands, the only home she had ever known, had fallen.

*

William Keagan received the news in the days following that all had gone according to plan on Clovis's front. He was pleased with the efforts of all of his men and celebrated extensively with Judith. Much to his pleasure, his wife was particularly aroused when she heard the news. She told him that she felt like a queen in the Murrieta, a feeling she had considered only a dream during her time in the crowded cities of the East. Even with the wealth she had, there was nothing like the power that they were beginning to acquire. He was elated that she felt that way, as it was one more affirmation of his success.

With Daniel seizing economic control of the Riverlands, and Clovis amassing an army in the south, it was now time for William to take the next step to turn their operation into an empire. He assembled his confidantes in his study. Judith, of course, was already briefed on everything he was going to explain.

"My friends," William greeted, as he looked at Cassius, Gregory,

Collin, Frankie, and Henry in turn. "I've assembled y'all here to discuss the next step in our conquest. As y'all may or may not have already heard, Clovis's mission was a success. The V'ahani of the Riverlands have been successfully displaced from their home and are under our control at the Hold. With all the work we've done here, we'll now have a firm grip on all dealings south of the Riverlands, which as y'all know is nearly three-quarters of the entire Murrieta."

"William, that's marvelous to hear, my boy," Henry praised. "You should be so very proud of this accomplishment!"

"Indeed," Cassius added. "It seems everything went fairly closely to plan."

"So what's our next move?" Gregory asked.

This question in particular made William light up. He knew he was a brilliant schemer and strategy was something he enjoyed even more than the resulting action. "I'm glad you asked! As I've said, we have a vast sum of this territory controlled now, but the Mountainlands and its Fortress remain in the hands of the V'ahani. Once Daniel feels that he's won the people over in the Riverlands, and Clovis deems his army fit to attack, we'll then move north day-by-day until it's all ours. We should now have the resources to force our will upon the V'ahani that remain."

"Brilliant," Henry gushed.

"Which brings me to the next steps for the people in this room," William continued. "My ultimate goal is not just to handle all trade in the Murrieta, but to also connect this territory to the great eastern cities from which we came and take a cut of every bit of economic prosperity that comes from that connection. In order to facilitate this, Judith, Henry, and I will go back east, with the assistance of Cassius, to see my father. If there is anyone that can provide us such a partnership it will be him. Once he sees what I've done here, there will be no way for him to deny how lucrative this can be. I'll set forth terms, and we'll have all that we desire!"

Even the thought that he could be close to achieving what he felt was his life's purpose had William giddy.

"But Billy, I should go with you," Gregory pleaded. "The journey east is dangerous and I should be there to ensure your safety."

William turned to him. "You're one of my closest confidantes, Gregory," he said. "For that reason, I need you here to assume my post in my absence. This is the most important role of any in our organization. I need you to ensure that Clovis and Daniel succeed in their exploits and that we also maintain that which we have acquired thus far. Also, I need you to look after our family that remains here in Fayette. As for Collin and Frankie, y'all are to assist Gregory in any way he might require. Can I trust y'all to be up to this task?"

"Sir, I swear to you that it shall be done," Gregory promised as the others nodded appreciatively.

"Great, thank you," William gestured. "We must be off now, my friends. I hope to see y'all very soon and when I do, we'll be rich beyond y'all's wildest dreams."

With that, Judith, Henry, William, and Cassius were off to make preparations for the coming journey back east. He knew it would present its challenges, but all he could hope for was that things continue to go the Keagans' way.

The snow fell softly now on the mountainside. Besides the faint whisper of the wind, there was not a sound to be heard. It was as if the Mother had nothing left to say after all that had occurred within Her domain. Now Hanzah lay in Her hands, barely holding on to whatever life remained inside of him. The winter cold had his body so numb that he was no longer aware of the pain from his broken arm. In fact, he had lost almost all feeling in the rest of his limbs, as well. As he lay there, now awake in the snow, he prayed for the safety of his new friends. They were all he thought about despite his current predicament. He would have gladly accepted that this was the end for him, if he could simply know that they would be all right. He'd endured too much loss, and he hoped that this would be the end of it.

After some time of shivering and pondering in solitude, the swallow he had seen earlier had returned to him. The little bird landed in the exact same spot on the tree above him, shaking off some of the dusty snow as it reached its perch. Hanzah was glad that he was once again not alone.

"Hello th-there," he whispered in his shivery, chattering voice. His words were hardly audible in his current state. "Th-thank you f-for coming back." The swallow stared at him and did not make a sound, but it did not matter to Hanzah. He was just happy with the sight of a familiar face. "D-did you find them?"

Finally, the swallow responded. "Alive. Together," it hissed back.

Hanzah was overcome with joy. His friends were well, at least for now, and he had company.

Unfortunately for him, it was not meant to last. In the distance, a faint sound could be heard, which scared the swallow off. This was devastating for Hanzah.

"N-no! C-come back!" he begged, beginning to cry. As much as he knew he should be worried about whatever it was that was approaching him, he wasn't. Whether it was something that wanted to eat him or simply the wind, all Hanzah wanted was to not be alone in his last moments.

He thought about his father, as the sound grew nearer. A memory came to him from a time that he was lost in the woods near his people's camp. Latera and he had been playing a game of hide-and-seek in which he had inadvertently fallen into a ditch. As he lay here in the snow now, he remembered hearing the voice of his father echoing through the woods then, calling out his name. "HANZAH!" he remembered hearing with tremendous vibrato.

As he lay in the quiet of the mountain, beginning to feel dizzy, he replied aloud in a whisper, "I am here."

Again and again, his father called out to him from his memory, "Hanzah! Where are you?!"

As loudly as he could, as if his father would be able to hear him now, he yelled in a hoarse voice, "I am here!"

Suddenly, someone came running over to him, causing him to jump out of his daze. When Hanzah realized that he was no longer in a memory, he continued crying, but out of fear.

"My boy, do not cry, it will be all right. Everything is going to be all right. You are safe now," the man standing over him promised.

Hanzah tried his best to see through his blurry eyes and struggled to remain calm. When he had finally relaxed, he was able to see who it was standing above him. A smile spread across his face as he whispered, "Uncle Orrin, you found me."

~

CURIOUS ABOUT WHAT HAPPENS NEXT?

Continue to Amazon to buy the next book in the series now:

https://www.amazon.com/author/nbaustin

Need more than that?
Check out Nicholas Austin's website!

linktr.ee/nbaustinbooks

ABOUT THE AUTHOR

N.B. Austin is the author, screenwriter, and blogger behind the Civilands Series. *Crimson River*, his first novel, was a finalist for the *2016-2017 BooksGoSocialDaily Book of the Year Award*.

Based in Austin, Texas, but hailing originally from Long Island, New York. University of Texas at Austin educated. His experience as writer and editor for several scholastic newsletter publications combined with a passion for song writing, soon inspired him to divert his attention to storytelling.

Find more about N.B. Austin, including his blog and details on free book giveaways, at:

linktr.ee/nbaustinbooks

www.ingramcontent.com/pod-product-compliance
Lightning Source LLC
Chambersburg PA
CBHW020058180626
46812CB00006B/2388